FORBIDDEN POWER
PART II

By

Paul Kyriazi

www.PaulKyriazi.com

Forbidden Power - Part II

Forbidden Power the movie is *Part One* of this story.
It is available on Amazon & Vimeo.

Winner of **28** International Awards Including:

2018 - Las Vegas International Action on Film Mega-Fest, competing with over 600 movies:

BEST YOUNG PERFORMER - Kaiya Grey
BEST SPECIAL EFFECTS - Aaron Amort & Preston Sawyer

2018 - International BITB Hollywood Film Festival, competing with over 1,000 movies:

BEST PICTURE - Forbidden Power
BEST DIRECTOR - Paul Kyriazi
BEST ACTOR - Lincoln Bevers
BEST ACTRESS - Nasanin Nuri

2019 - London Flicks Festival:

BEST THRILLER - Forbidden Power
BEST ACTOR - Lincoln Bevers.
BEST ACTRESS - Nasanin Nuri
BEST SUPPORTING ACTRESS - Hannah Janssen
BEST PRODUCERS - Bruce Dowling - Jan Van Tassell - Conrad Denke - Harry Mok

2019 - BEST SCIENCE FICTION - Oklahoma BB Film Festival

2019 - BEST ORIGINAL SCREENPLAY- Florence Film Awards Italy

2019 - BEST FEATURE FILM - New York Cinematography Awards

2019 - BEST FEATURE LONG NARRATIVE - American Golden Picture International Film Festival Jacksonville, Florida.

2019 - BEST DIRECTOR - Diamond Film Awards Battipaglia Italy

2019 - BEST SCIENCE FICTION - International Festigious Awards Los Angeles

2019 - BEST PRODUCED SCREENPLAY - Los Angeles Independent Film Festival Awards

2019 - BEST SCIENCE FICTION FEATURE FILM - Horror Bowl Sci-If Festival INDIA

2019 - BEST ORIGINAL SCREENPLAY - Hollywood Blood Horror Festival

2019 - BEST SCIENCE FICTION - Oniros Festival - Saint Vincent Italy

2019 - Global Film Festival Awards Los Angeles
BEST PRODUCED SCREENPLAY - Paul Kyriazi
BEST SUPPORTING ACTRESS - Hannah Janssen
BEST TRAILER - Jon-Paul Durant

2019 - Los Angeles Film Awards
BEST SCIENCE FICTION

2019 - American Filmatic Arts Awards New York
BEST SCIENCE FICTION FEATURE

2020 - Best Actor Awards Aosta, Italy
BEST SUPPORTING ACTOR - Harry Mok

2020 - New York Movie Awards
BEST ORIGINAL SCREENPLAY

4

CHAPTER 1

1

"Mr. President, anyone who can cross millions of miles of space, will be able to take care of themselves when they get here.

Don't start a *'shoot-them-down'* policy that you can't finish."

Albert Einstein to President Truman - July 19, 1952

Why they had traveled so far to reach earth, only to impregnate their energy into a little Native American girl, residents of said planet would never know. Why they had chosen to hover over the meteor crater in Arizona until they chose the right human receptacle, would also remain a mystery. One thing the little girl did reveal, when she became an adult: "We have liquidated worlds."

"You can cruise off and hide, but sooner or later you'll have to join in order to survive."

Michaelson's words didn't have the effect on George Barrett that the egomaniacal man was hoping for. George and his three friends had made it to the boat, regardless of the bullets fired at them.

Holding onto the railing, George let out a quiet "Never," knowing that with the distance that Michaelson was standing on shore, and the sound of the boat powering up, Michaelson would never hear it.

As the boat left the pier, heading north into Seattle's Elliot Bay, George kept his eye on Elaine, Michaelson's head of security that was standing next to him. She had already fired shots at him and his group and seemed ready to fire a Hail-Mary bullet at him.

Finally, she and Michaelson returned to the car, ready to get back to their business: city, then state, then country domination. And with the country, the world would abide.

As part-time boatman and full-time fixer, Patrico Serrano, steered the boat north, George and his friends climbed the ladder to the upper deck. George and Cathy took the port-side bench, with Chang and Angela gratefully sitting down on the starboard side.

Cathy had been kidnapped by Michaelson's group and held captive until George and Chang came to rescue her. Now, looking at George, she wanted answers to what was happening. But she decided to wait until they were alone.

Angela was looking at the wound on her husband's shoulder. There was good muscle there to keep the bullet from causing too much damage from the angle it had entered. Married only six months to a woman who was half Chang's fifty years, their relationship had turned into a comfortable situation for both. Angela rescued off the streets. Chang, out of prison and trying to lead a straightforward life.

The four sat in silence gazing over the waters as Patrico piloted them on to Vancouver. "How long till we get there?" George called to him.

"About three hours."

"Get where?" Cathy asked.

"Vancouver," George said.

"I can't go there. I've got ..."

"We have no choice for now."

"You'd better start telling me what's going on. I've been dragged out of my house, chased and shot at without having any idea of ..."

"Just let me catch my breath, will ya? We'll get to Vancouver, think things out and if you want to come back here, you can."

"I'm coming back all right and heading straight to the police."

"I don't think that's a good idea, but I'll explain later."

"I think it's about time to give that package the deep six," Patrico said swiveling his chair towards George.

George nodded, stood up and reluctantly descended the ladder to the lower deck. This was not going to be easy; dumping the dead body of the most sensual woman he'd ever been with, if woman she was. What part of her was still Chumana the Native American human? What part of her was an alien entity that had taken over her mind and body when she was a child?

He slowly stepped down into the cabin where she laid, sheet covered. The blood from the bullet that he had fired into her brain made the top of the sheet half red.

Hesitant to take action, George sat down on the cushioned sofa across from the dead woman. He laid back and momentarily shut his eyes, then opened them. *I have to do this quickly*, he thought.

He stood up and knelt in front of her. As he moved his hands under her to pick her up, Veronica's bare arm fell out of the sheet towards him, like she was beckoning. He ran his hand over the skin of her arm, flawless save for a curious tattoo.

Should he take one last look at that beautiful face? Even in death, would that face of hers still be able to seduce him?

He slowly reached for the part of the sheet that was covering her head. He pulled on it to reveal her face. Her eyes flicked open. Her mouth let out a scream as she lunged for him, getting her hands around his neck and pushing him back onto the opposite sofa. Her scream got louder. He couldn't breathe.

His eyes open. He woke up on the sofa alone. Looking over to the other sofa, he saw Veronica's body still wrapped in the sheet.

How long had he slept? Cathy came down the stairs into the cabin, followed by Chang and Angela. She sat down next to George putting her hand on his shoulder. "What's wrong?"

George kept his eyes transfixed on the sheet-covered Veronica. "She's alive."

Chang moved the sheet back from Veronica's face. "She's dead."

Patrico, leaving the boat on automatic, came down to the cabin to see what the problem was, but couldn't understand what was going on.

"It's okay," Cathy assured George. But he didn't hear her. He was lost in thought.

4

Patrico came back to the upper deck, sat down on the pilot's chair, turned off the autopilot, and gripped the wheel. He preferred the feeling of the waves fighting the rudder to letting the navigational system have all the fun.

Chang and Angela soon joined him. They sat down and remained silent until Cathy finally climbed up the ladder.

"What's he doing down there?" Chang asked.

Cathy sat down. "He wouldn't explain about the body. But finally said he's going to take care of it. And wants to do it alone."

Chang nodded. "The sooner we get rid of that body the better I'll like this pleasure cruise."

"And what a cruise," Angela added sarcastically.

"Who is that woman?" Cathy asked.

"I only know a little about it," Chang said. "Better to let George tell you, when he's ready."

"Well, somebody better tell me what this is all about," Cathy said, "and soon." She could see that Chang had said all he wanted to on the subject, so she leaned back on the seat to calm down.

After a few minutes, Chang went to the ladder to check on George. Looking down he saw him standing by the side of the boat holding Veronica's sheeted body. "You'd better weight her down with something first," Chang called down. "We don't want her to float back into town."

George looked up and nodded at Chang. He laid Veronica down on the stern bench, ascended the ladder, walked over to Patrico and said, "You'd better take care of the body after we get off. And put something on it to make it sink."

Patrico looked up at George. "After you get off? Hey man, I'm not cruising into Vancouver with a dead body."

"And neither am I."

"What are you talking about?"

George pulled out his phone and started searching for something. "I'm not going to Vancouver."

Cathy stood up. "Oh, no George. Now what?"

"I already know what he's thinking," Chang said.

George turned to him. "Do you?"

"Yes. You don't like this terrorist bullshit any more than I do."

"What?" Angela asked.

Chang looked out over the ocean. "Jimmy Castellanos."

Angela stood up next to Chang. "Who's he?"

"A friend who died on 9-11."

Angela's fears where confirmed. "Oh, no."

Chang turned from the ocean and looked at his wife. "Nobody tells me to cruise off and hide. Nobody."

"Exactly," George agreed.

"Are we going back?" Cathy asked.

George ignored her and turned to Patrico. "Twenty-three miles north of here is an abandoned pier. I want you to stop there."

"What are you doing?" Cathy asked.

"Yeah, good, I'm with you," Chang said to George. "And I think we...."

Angela grabbed Chang's good arm and turned him toward her. "Wait a minute. We pack up, risk our lives and now we're going back?"

"Hold on, guys," Patrico jumped in. You want me to drop you two off and take the women on to ..."

"He's not taking me anywhere without you," Angela said to Chang.

"You'll get to Vancouver in a couple of hours, right?" Chang said to Patrico.

"Sure," Patrico said.

Chang turned to George. "You said you had money for all of us?"

"Yeah, cash and credit cards right in my pocket.'

"Hey, don't give away my twenty grand," Patrico said.

"Don't worry," George said, searching on his phone again. "I've got that covered."

"This is crazy," Cathy said. "Why are you doing this?"

"If I do nothing," George said, without looking up from his phone, "Michaelson's group will keep on expanding until they take over everything."

Cathy shook her head. "Whoever they are, you can't stop a group like that."

"We can blow the hell out of his place," Chang said. "Dynamite his ass."

George turned to Chang. "No, he's got groups in four different places. Not only Seattle."

"Wait a minute," Angela said. "You two can't take them on."

"The hell we can't," Chang said. "You know, I've already got a half-baked idea of what we can do."

"Stop this, George," Cathy said in a voice barely audible over the engine's roar. "We should just get away from here, like you said. And then decide things."

Patrico switched the boat to autopilot and stood up. "What's it gonna be, folks? I got to get this boat back and I want my 20 grand."

George held out his phone to Patrico who gave him a quizzical look and then took it.

George pointed to the display screen. "Just head for those co-ordinates."

5

According to George's phone map, the deserted pier that Patrico was now tying up the boat to was forty-eight miles north of Seattle. At the stern, the two couples continued their debate.

George, even with his enhanced mind and body was beginning to weaken under Cathy's barrage of arguments. He was beginning to wonder if their sexual contact over the past months had the same effect on her that Veronica's sexual contact had on him. Could Veronica's power be passed on via other hosts? Or could victims be empowered only from the source, namely Veronica?

He hadn't noticed any empowered traits from Cathy in the last weeks, except maybe for the fact that she had stopped complaining about his extended lovemaking. And she quickly became skilled at firing the pistol that Chang had given her during her rescue.

George eyed Cathy for signs of empowerment as she spoke. "It's not up to you, George. You can't tell me what to do."

"Same goes for me," Angela piped in.

"You're my wife," Chang said. "I'm responsible for you. And it's best for you to go on to Vancouver and meet there, when I'm finished here."

"You saved me in that alley," Angela said, "and I'm grateful. But I won't wait someplace to hear if you're alive or dead."

Chang gave a painful shrug, due to his wound. "She's got a point," he said to George.

"Exactly," Cathy said.

Standing by the bow, rope in hand, Patrico called out. "What's it going to be boys and girls? I gotta get this boat back."

"Alright," George finally agreed. "Let's stay together for now. We can work this out once we get to a motel."

Chang nodded and motioned for Angela to deboard. She grabbed the handle of her small roller suitcase.

"You gonna drag that thing all over hell?" Chang calmly asked her.

"I'm not going to fight terrorists without my lipstick." She stepped off the boat pulling her suitcase after her.

"You're not fighting any terrorists, at all," Chang said following her.

"Hey George, where's my money?" Patrico asked tossing the rope on the boat.

George stepped off the boat and then grabbed a wad of cash from his jacket. "This should hold you for now."

Patrico grabbed the cash and thumbed through it. "Screw 'hold me'. I want it all now."

"I need what I have on me. I'll make a bank run soon and pay you the rest later. And a little more."

"Oh, come on. Don't do this to me. I need to ..."

"We'll eventually need that ride to Vancouver, so keep your phone on loud."

Patrico stuffed the cash into his jacket pocket and moved to the stern rope. "I'm not picking you up until I get the full twenty grand for this trip and money in advance for the next."

"I'll have it for sure," George assured him. "When we meet here, I'll hand you thirty grand before we set foot on the boat. Just make sure that when I call, you come running ... or cruising ... or whatever you call it."

"Cruising," Patrico said, jumping back on board.

"And about that package in the cabin ..."

"Don't worry. I'll weigh her down enough to keep her with the fish forever."

"A couple miles out, right?"

"I know my job, George."

"Okay. It might be a couple of days, or a couple of weeks, so keep your phone charged up."

"Got it," Patrico said climbing the ladder to the top deck. "Stay healthy. At least till you get me my money."

"If something happens to me," I send it along with the girls."

"Just as long as it gets to me," Patrico said looking down on George with a serious face. But then gave him a slight smile, "But I hope you'll be handing the cash to me yourself." He gunned the engines in reverse and started backing away from the pier.

"Is this where your plan ends?" Cathy asked George as he punched some letters into his phone.

"Looks like a storm's moving in," Chang said. "And it'll be dark in a couple of hours. How about we at least get off this rotten pier safely?"

"Right," George answered as he scrolled down his display screen. "It is kind of wobbly. Be careful."

"And then what?" Cathy asked George.

"I hope you're not allergic to dogs."

"What's dogs got to do with anything?" she asked as she slowly followed Chang and Angela on the pier to the beach.

I guess her mind hasn't been empowered, George thought. *Otherwise, she could have figured that out.*

14

6

From the upper deck wheel seat, Patrico looked back at the shrinking shoreline. He was only a half-mile out and would wait another couple of miles before he would idle the engines, wrap Veronica's body in chains and deep-six her.

From his viewpoint, Patrico couldn't see the green glow that was beginning to show through the sheet Veronica was wrapped in. The pulsating light started in her brain and then slowly expanded to luminate her whole body.

It was the same green light that came from the alien hand that had victimized her as a little girl, taking over her life. Now that light, that had managed to remain after the bullet to the head had snuffed out her body, was doing its job of rejuvenation.

Under the sheet, still in her snakeskin dress, Veronica's hand twitched. Next her eyes slowly opened. Seeing the white of the sheet, the energy that was driving her knew it was something that needed escaping from.

The pulsating energy gave her body enough power to squirm out of its confinement. It animated her enough to sit up and plant her still sheet-wrapped feet onto the deck.

Controlling Veronica like a marionette, the energy pulled the stings inside of her to stand. Using her eyes, it looked around at the sea and then the ladder in front of her that went to the upper deck. Now, there was enough power for Veronica to come slightly to her Darwinian senses.

She approached the ladder and grabbed the rung in front of her. She began to slowly climb up. She stopped climbing when her head was high enough to see Patrico piloting the boat with his back to her.

Climbing back down to the deck, she turned and saw the shoreline. She knew, that with the energy's help, she could make it there.

She took a step toward the railing, but the energy made her stop. She was missing something. What? Her left hand reached down to grab the handle of the lizard skin bag that Patrico had wrapped up with her dead body. It held her Navajo doll. George had given the doll to Patrico to dump into the sea with her. It was evidence of a killing that they didn't want to leave behind.

Now with her doll and enough reptilian brain power to operate her body, Veronica stepped up on the bench seat next to the railing and jumped into the water.

The small part of her brain that was functioning as a human thought she was having a drowning nightmare. But the alien energy drove her on with one-armed dogpaddling, kicking and jerking her head up for gasps of air.

Her left hand knew its job and kept a firm grip on the bag which held her doll. Her controlling energy knew its importance.

Finally, Veronica floated to a stand and waded onto the beach. Fifty yards in front of her was a dense forest. She headed for it with no reason except to go forward. Then, with her body needing more rejuvenation, the energy from within let Veronica *Chumana* Hawthorne age 28, fall to the sand unconscious.

CHAPTER 2

1

Nineteen years earlier, Veronica, then named Chumana He-Crow, age nine, guided her two Navajo girlfriends through the darkness of the Arizona desert. She held her tribal doll tightly to her side. The doll's face, that of an angry old man, had the same concentrated eyes that Chumana had as she headed towards her midnight destination.

"I think we should be getting back," eight-year-old Little Bird urged Chumana.

"My father's gonna beat me if I get back late," ten-year-old Odina said.

Chumana looked back at Odina. "Your father won't be doing anything to you after tonight."

"Who's going to stop him?"

"You will."

Little Bird slowed her walk. "We've been to the crater a hundred times."

Chumana waved her hand forward. "But not at night."

"What's so special about seeing it at night," Little Bird asked.

Odina jumped in, "It means the coyotes are out."

"They won't hurt us," Chumana said.

The two girls, who always did Chumana's bidding followed her into the night.

Twenty minutes later, the three came to the edge of the Barringer meteor crater, named after its discoverer. In the dark, the other side of the rim, a half-mile away, was almost invisible. The bottom, 700 feet down, was just as hard to see.

"I love this place," Chumana said sitting down on a rock made pock-marked by the meteor that blasted it 50,000 years ago.

"You love it? Why?" Odina asked as she and Little Bird sat down on other rocks.

"I was born here two years ago," Chumana said.

Her two friends looked at each other trying to understand her statement.

Chumana moved the hand holding her doll inside the miniature blanket that wrapped it. Once under the blanket, she pressed down with her palm, onto something inside.

"How long are we gonna be out here?" Odina asked.

Chumana slowly turned her head and looked at the two girls. Holding them in a steady gaze, she slowly said, "Why don't you sleep awhile?"

Their eyes becoming heavy, the two girls moved from their rocks, laid down on the desert dirt, and feel asleep. That task completed, Chumana looked up at the star-filled sky and waited.

Ten minutes passed without Chumana moving a muscle. Suddenly she heard what sounded like a Navajo ceremonial rattle instrument at her feet. With lightning speed, her left hand snatched up the head of the rattlesnake that was attracted to the warmth of her feet.

Holding its head in the milking position, she brought the reptile close to her face to examine it. She put her right hand under its fang baring open mouth. Not minding that it was wrapping itself around her arm, she pressed down on its head. Two drops of venom came out of the snake's fangs landing in the palm of her hand.

Tiring of the snake's hissing, she tossed it violently over the edge of the crater. She moved her hand toward her mouth and licked the snake's poison just to satisfy her curiosity about its taste. Her name, Chumana meant *Snake Maiden*, so she figured that *what she was one of, could not harm her.*

Besides, she had the *power from above* in her from two years ago when she was touched by the *one from above's* hand. That power nullified any threat that a crawling reptile could muster.

More than an hour passed at the crater when Chumana finally shook her two friends out of their hypnotically induced slumber.

"He's here," Chumana said, like she was announcing the arrival of an ice cream truck salesman.

"What?" Little Bird asked slowly sitting up.

Odina opened her eyes. "What's going on?"

When Little Bird saw the seven-foot, green-skinned creature she froze with terror. Her open mouth gave out only a silent scream.

Odina, first looked at Chumana who has a smile like she had just discovered a hidden cookie jar. Then, she saw the tall shape that was reaching out for her. As the thing grabbed her, Odina's scream was anything but silent.

The hideous face of the alien showed no sympathy as it placed its three-fingered hand on Odina's head, and pulsated green energy into her brain.

18

Little Bird moved to run, but Chumana grabbed and held her immobile until it was her turn. Her turn came after Odina hit the desert floor unconscious.

Chumana pushed Little Bird into the long arms of the alien to be indoctrinated. She looked on with calm glee as Little Bird struggled, but then went limp as the creature impregnated her brain.

2

Two months later, Chamana's father drove her from their Arizona Navajo reservation to Winslow in his beat-up jeep. Winslow is famous for its *Standing on the Corner* statue to honor the Eagles' song *Take It Easy*. With less than 2,000 families living there, all shoppers are welcomed. But not so much Chumana's often drunk father, Jackson He-Crow.

Still, he ignored the cold shoulder given him when he came to town every two weeks to buy supplies. He often took his nine-year-old daughter with him, to soften the bad treatment the locals gave him. The locals weren't so much against Indians, just drunken ones. And Jackson held the gold in that competition.

Jackson got gas for his jeep, filled his propane bottle and now, holding hands with Chumana, crossed the street to Sam's General Store.

It had been three months since Chumana and her two friends returned from their late night visit to the meteor crater. All three of their fathers were inclined to beat them. All three of their fathers, belt in hand, took a long look into each of their daughter's eyes and decided to let them off without even a warning. *One does not stare into the eyes of the Gorgon too long, for fear of turning to stone.*

As Jackson and Chumana approached the store, Little Bird and Odina came out licking on candy canes. Seeing Chumana, both girls greeted her with a smile and a 'Hello Chumana'.

Jackson slowed his walking and stared at the two little girls. They stared back. Jackson got the message. He wasn't sure of the message's meaning, but he knew it was bad, so he proceeded into the store, pulling Chumana along with him.

"You stay away from those two," Jackson said to his daughter as they entered. "Something's not right with them."

"There's nothing wrong with them," Chumana said softly, but defiantly.

Jackson knew not to argue with her since she was seven years old. Since that first night when she returned from the meteor crater, two years ago. She came back at four in the morning with a look that Jackson had only seen in rattlesnake eyes that had often invaded his home.

A shotgun blast took care of the rattlesnakes. But to take care of Chumana, Jackson figured that, if he ever pointed a shotgun at her, she'd have him turn it on himself and teach him what the flash of the double-barrels looked like, just before their load hit him in his face.

No, he didn't need that kind of action at all. Better to be nice to his daughter and save the beatings for his wife.

Looking around the old-style general store, Jackson saw the usual old guys hanging around. Two guys throwing darts, one reading a girlie magazine, two drinking from brown-bag covered bottles.

To Jackson, they looked like yahoos in a badly cast movie, character actors too much in character to be believed.

"Make it quick, Jackson," Sam, the owner behind the counter, said. "Grab the wampum you need, pay and hit the road." Sam was one of those *Injuns are okay, as long as they're not drunk* kind of guy.

"Sure," Jackson said without eyeing him.

Chumana gave Sam the same look that she had given that rattlesnake, indifference.

"What are you lookin' at, little papoose?"

Chumana let it go. She had larger plans than to deal with simpletons.

Jackson walked over to Sam at the checkout counter. "Give me a bottle of that Duggan's Dew, please."

Sam purposely took his time reacting. "Kind of strong for you, ain't it, Jackson?"

"I can handle it."

"Seems like you should be tapering off for a while."

Chumana turned her back to Sam and pretended to be interested in the dart game that the two men were playing.

"I'm taking it home," Jackson told Sam. "It's mostly for guests."

Sam turned and reached for a bottle on the shelf behind him. "I'll bet."

"Just ring it up, please."

"I'll ring it up when I'm good and ready."

"Any trouble there, Sam?" The dart player named Bob called over.

"I'm not sure," Sam said. "Are you causing trouble, Jackson?"

"No. No trouble. I'm just in kind of a hurry."

"You let me know if there's any trouble," Bob said.

Sam shook his head at Jackson. "On thing a big fire-water drinker like you should never be, and that's *in a hurry*."

"What?"

"Driving, even walking is dangerous for a drunk," Sam said.

"I'm not a drunk. I'm just gonna take this bottle home."

"All right then. That's a good boy."

Chumana left Jackson's side and walked over to Bob. Jackson turned to see what she was up to.

When Bob saw the skinny little Chumana approaching him with eyes that were ready to strike, he didn't know what to think. "Hey, Jackson. You'd better tell this little squaw of yours to stop eyeballin' me."

Chumana stopped in front of Bob, looked up at him, and held out her hand, palm up.

Bob sputtered a chuckle. "I ain't giving you any money."

"Darts," she said.

"You want a game, do you?"

"Let's finish our game first," Bob's partner said.

"Wait a minute, Jimmy," Bob said. "It looks like I've just been challenged."

Chumana smiled.

"How about a nickel a point?" Bob said.

Chumana shook her head. "Best of five darts for twenty."

Bob looked over at his three friends. They were no longer interested in nude magazine photos or beer. They wanted to see what Bob would do.

"Hell, I don't mind taking wampum from a baby," Bob said. "Here you go, honey," he pulled three darts out of the board and handed them to her, as well as the two he was holding. "You first." He turned to his friends and said, "This I gotta see. She'll be lucky to hit the ..."

Hearing the first dart hit, Bob turned to the board to see Chumana had thrown a bullseye. "What that ...?"

"Did you see that?" Sam said to Jackson.

Three more bullseyes and one just off center followed in quick order. "You're turn," Chumana said.

Bob's three friends started to give him the horselaugh, but he cut them off with a quick, mean look.

"Your turn, Bob," Chumana repeated.

"Yeah, it's your turn, Bob," Jimmy said snickering.

Bob stood there like a bewildered Custer at Little Big Horn.

"I've never seen anything like that," the girlie magazine reader said.

"That ain't right," Sam said.

Bob walked over to the dart board to examine the darts. Then he turned back to Chumana. "What the hell are you?"

"Play or pay," she said quietly.

Bob walked over next to her and looked down at the top of her head. "I'll tell you what. I don't feel like playing and I ain't gonna ..."

The pain that shot through Bob's fingers hit his brain faster than the time he accidently hit his fingers with a hammer. And it was a different kind of pain. A weird kind. "All right," he groaned out. "Let me get to my wallet."

Chumana let go of his fingers. Bob painfully got to his wallet and held it open in front of Chumana. She looked inside, saw a twenty and pulled it out. Then she turned and walked over to her now proud father and handed him the bill.

"Damned red devil," Bob said to her back.

Chumana slowly turned. Bob took a step back as he heard her say, "Just wait till I'm thirteen. I'll really be a handful then."

Jackson turned to Bob and said confidently, "I'll have a *large* bottle of that Dugan's Dew firewater."

"Sure thing, Mister He-Crow," Sam said turning and reaching for a larger bottle than before. "That's quite a daughter you have there."

"Any problems with us Injuns coming in here, Sam?" Jackson asked.

Bob looked at Chumana. "No, Jackson. Not at all."

"Jackson?"

"I mean Mister He-Crow."

"You should have seen me in town today," Jackson said to his tiny wife Neddy. "I really showed those *son-of-a-bitches*."

"Oh," she smiled weakly. "What happened?"

Chumana sitting next to her father at their old, wooden, kitchen table, looked at him curiously.

Jackson could feel her look, but continued bragging, "I made them toe the line. That's what happened."

"How so?" Neddy asked.

Jackson looked down on Chumana. "Well, actually our little girl here, scared the hell out them by winning a dark game. We won some money and then ..."

"How much money," Neddy asked.

"None of your business."

Neddy went back to eating.

4

A few weeks later, Jackson woke up to the sound of someone talking coming from outside his open bedroom window. His head, still spinning from last night's drinking, he managed to get to his feet and look out the window.

He saw nothing but darkness and the shack that a young couple had rented from him. The lights went on there, so he figured that Charlie Hawkins and his wife Koko heard the talking, too.

Neddy sat up in her bed across the room. "What's that noise?"

"I'll take care of it," Jackson told her. "Go back to sleep."

Not minding his ragged underwear and T-shirt, Jackson walked into his living room and turned on the light. He saw that the front door was open. He grabbed the double-barrel shotgun that was leaning on the wall and went outside.

"Anything wrong," Charlie called from the front of his shack.

Jackson turned to see him and Koko standing there. "I'm not sure," he called back. The strange talking continued. Now it sounded like a one-sided conversation, with whoever was speaking, listening to somebody, and then responding.

Then, ten yards ahead, Jackson saw his daughter sitting on the ground, leaning on a tree stump. Letting his shotgun hang down by his side he called to Charlie and his wife, "It's okay. It's just my kid."

Charlie waved, put his arm around Koko and went back inside their shack. Jackson approached Chumana. He felt like giving her hell for disturbing everyone but knew better.

Chumana was looking up into the night sky filled with stars. Jackson tried to discern her talking, but she wasn't making sense in English or Navajo. Jackson approached, his bare feet not making a sound.

Without turning around Chumana said, "Hello, Papa."

"What are you doing out here?"

"Nothing."

"Who are you talking to?"

"Just my doll," motioning to it held in her arm.

"What is he saying?"

"He doesn't talk, Papa. He's just a doll."

"So, you're talking for both of you, I guess."

"My friends talk to me."

"What friends?"

"The star people."

Jackson knelt next to her. "You know when I was a boy, I talked with wolves."

"What did you talk about?"

"Oh, things. Things on my mind." He put his arm around her. "You know, I want to tell you something important. You see that dead tree out there? The one on the right?"

"Yes."

"Well, I buried something there for you. Something nice, for when you're grown up."

Chumana stared at the tree in the distance. "What is it?"

"It's a kind of treasure," Jackson said.

"A treasure? Like gold and things."

"You'll find out when you're grown up. It's buried about three feet deep, so you'll have to dig and dig."

"But can't you tell me what it is?"

"It's a nice surprise. That's all I can tell you now." Jackson stood up. "So how about coming back inside and to bed to dream about gold and things?"

"I will in a while, Papa. I promise."

"Okay, my little snake maiden. Don't stay out too long or the wolves might eat you."

"If they try, they'll be sorry."

"Yes," Jackson said, heading back inside. "I guess they would be sorry.

CHAPTER 3

1

Twenty-eight-year-old Veronica *Chumana* Hawthorne felt her shoulder shaking as she lay on the dark beach. How long had she laid there unconscious until this intrusion? She didn't know.

She could feel the sand she was lying on but had no knowledge of who she was or how she got there. She could hardly tell if she was alive or not. The shaking persisted.

"Miss. Miss," the sound came to her. *What is that?* She thought. *An enemy?* She opened her eyes and jerked her head up to ascertain the danger. A blurred image. Not a dangerous animal. A human. But maybe dangerous.

"Can you get up?" came a man's voice.

Veronica could see the man taking a few steps back to give her space. She got to her knees and looked around with jerky head movements. *The sea, a beach, a forest. And a man,* Veronica's semi-conscious human brain deduced.

As she got to her feet, she could feel something drag on the sand. She looked down at the lizard bag that was still clutched in her left hand. The head of the Navajo doll was sticking out of the bag. Seeing it brought her some comfort.

The middle-aged man looked over the snakeskin-dressed beauty in front of him. The wet snake scales looked like fish scales to him. Was she a mermaid washed ashore? Her perfectly shaped, tanned legs told him no. "What happened to you?" he asked.

Veronica's eyes focused on him. Tall, clean-cut. Maybe not a threat.

"Did someone hurt you?"

Veronica was surprised when "No," escaped her lips. She could speak.

"Did you have trouble in the water?"

"Yes."

"Are there any of your friends here?"

She looked around, her motions still jerky. She shook her head to answer.

He took a step forward. She took an unbalanced step back. "Look, I'm no doctor, but you might be in shock. And this is no place to be while you're like this."

Veronica gave a jerky nod of the head.

"I'll tell what. My cabin is just a ten-minute walk from here. Up in the woods. Do you want to come with me, so you can gather your thoughts and call someone?"

If Veronica was cognitive, she might have smiled at *gather your thoughts*, since she had just recently had her thoughts blown from her brain by a .45 caliber pistol. The idea of going away from this place, appealed to her mind that was trying hard to reassemble its faculties. "Good," she reacted.

"Okay," the man said, reaching for her purse. "I'll help you with this."

Veronica hissed loudly and stepped back, clutching her purse to her chest.

"Okay, okay," he said freezing in his steps from her reptilian response. "The purse is all yours. Sorry, I didn't mean to ..." He pointed at the forest. "It's over here. Take your time. It's not far."

"Not far," she echoed, as she allowed her legs to move her forward.

2

"Here we are," the man said, pointing to his single floor cabin sitting alone in the thickly covered forest. Parked next to it on the dirt front yard was a blue SUV. Off about twenty feet was a paved one lane road.

Veronica was still unsteady on her feet as she followed the man up the four steps to the deck. He opened the door and stood back to let her enter first. She hesitated.

"It's alright. There's no one here. Just you and me."

She looked into the cabin as much as she could from where she was standing, to see if he was telling the truth. Finally, she reluctantly walked in.

"Well. Welcome to my home," the man said as he followed her inside.

"Home," she echoed as he closed the door behind them. She knew the meaning of *home* but couldn't remember one.

3

"Shut up," the veterinarian yelled at the two barking dogs that were caged up behind him. "Damned dogs," he said. "Don't know why I ever wanted to be in this profession."

"You said it would give you class," his wife said. "Remember?"

"Don't remind me," he said turning back to his human patient, Chang. The vet had a nice little home in the forest where he serviced the local cabin dweller's pets, as well as those in a couple of surrounding towns. His wife didn't have a license for treatment, but assisted with operations anyway, and ran the business end of his practice.

When George and his party arrived on foot at his home, the pet doctor was worried they were coming to raid his drug refrigerator, as they had no pets with them. So, he was relieved to be patching up their friend, instead of being robbed like he had been a few years ago by bikers.

Angela watched as the vet dug into Chang's arm in search of the bullet that had struck him during their escape. Chang was in great shape for a fifty-year-old but couldn't hide his pain when the vet pulled the bullet out. "Oh, Jesus."

"You chose this for us," Angela said to him.

Chang ignored her comment.

"You're lucky this hit you in the muscle at an oblique angle. It could have been bad."

"This isn't bad?" Chang asked grimacing.

"Are you sure you know what you're doing?" Angela asked the vet.

"Just let him do his work," Chang said.

"Lady," the vet said, without looking away from Chang's wound, "if he doesn't heal up nicely, you can come back and take any dog of your choice to replace him."

Angela's face contorted, "Hey, what kind of thing is ...?"

"You rang my doorbell," the vet interrupted. "I didn't ring yours."

"It'll be okay, dear," the vet's wife assured her.

George was standing next to Cathy watching the vet fix up his friend. Once the bullet was finally out of Chang, George walked into the next room, pulled out his phone and punched a name on it.

Before his cell phone rang in his downtown Seattle apartment, Miles, George's fired co-worker, felt nice and relaxed. George had given him thirty thousand dollars to start up a new company. And to celebrate, he had called Brenda, a blond co-worker from his old company to join him for dinner.

After they ate at an Italian restaurant, Miles had adroitly coaxed her to his apartment under the pretext of watching *Vertigo* on his 72 incher.

Brenda said that she had never seen the movie and let Miles convinced her that '*It's a must see tonight*'.

Actually, she had seen the movie, but she had a secret agenda that coincided with Miles', namely having some intimate companionship.

So, before James Steward could get Kim Novak into the sack, Miles and Brenda beat them to it with the soundtrack of the movie adding to the experience.

Now they sat at Mile's kitchen table sipping wine. Brenda bundled up in a soft white robe that Miles had stollen from a Hilton. Miles in his shorts and T-shirt.

"Bastard," Brenda said quietly.

Miles smiled with an expression that Don Juan might have had after a conquest. "Why do you say that?"

"This wasn't supposed to happen. I feel a little regretful."

"That's not how I feel."

"Oh, yeah? Exactly how do you feel, Miles?"

He looked at his wineglass, searched his mind and selected just the right compliment for blonds. "I feel like Kennedy, when Marilyn's dress hit the floor."

She didn't laugh. "Miles, are there no comedians in Seattle that you have to do stand up, after our lovemaking?"

"Speaking of stand up ..."

"You're vibrating."

"What?"

"Your phone in the other room."

"Oh, yeah. Excuse me," Miles got up and headed to the living room. He picked up his phone off the noisy, vibrating glass table, saw George's name lit up and punched it. "Yeah, George. What's up?"

"Did you deposit that cash I gave you?"

"No, not yet. It's still in the bag. Did you change your mind about our deal?"

"No, not at all, but I need that cash right now."

"What's going on?"

"I need you to grab the bag and start driving north with your phone on loud. I'll call you back when you get started."

"What? Right now? Hey, I can't ..."

"It's important, Miles. And I'll give you a few more thousand on top of that money when I return it to you. But it has to be tonight."

"Hey George, we're hardly friends and there's a big storm coming in about now, so ..."

"Look, Miles. I seldom hit the panic button, but I'm hitting it now and the answer to my problem is your help."

Miles looked over at Brenda sitting in the kitchen now looking at him and smiling. "George, I can't tell you what I'm giving up to do this for you, but it's a lot."

"I'll pay you back, Miles."

"You can't pay me back for what I'm losing, but I'll be there."

"Great. Don't forget to grab the bag."

"Right and keep my phone on loud."

"I'll call you when I get to a motel."

"What's this all ...?"

George hung up and went back into the vet's operating room.

"Get me ten Amoxicillin, will ya, hon?" The vet asked his wife.

George pulled out some cash from his jacket. "This is the cash I can give you now," he said to the vet who was wrapping Chang's arm with a bandage. George started searching on his phone as he spoke. "If you haven't contacted the police about us in a week, I'll send you more."

"Look, I'm not calling anybody," the vet said annoyed. "So, don't send me anything. I don't want to see or hear from you guys again."

"Right," George said looking up from his phone. "But we'll need you to drop us off at a motel about 20 minutes from here. If that's okay?"

"Anything to get rid of you people."

The vet's wife returned with a bottle of pills. "Here you go."

The vet took the bottle, checked the label and then handed it to Angela. "All right. This should stop any infection. See that he gets one of these, every four hours till they run out."

Angela took the bottle making a face. "Dog pills?"

"Don't knock 'em, honey," the vet said seriously. "The last one to take these, won *Best in Show*."

CHAPTER 4

1

"Thanks for the ride," George said to the vet as he, Cathy, Chang and Angela got out of the car at the Crazy Horse Cabin Motel. The storm that Miles had mentioned was now in full force with frequent displays of lightning and thunder.

"Just don't ask for any more favors, will ya," the vet said.

"Right." George closed the car door. The vet backed his car up, pointed it back to his wife and dogs and quickly disappeared in the rain and darkness.

The motel lobby was old, showing a lot of rotted wood. But at least it warmed up George and his companions while he used cash and phony names to get two cabins. The old lady manager didn't ask questions as she was used to couples checking in with cash at her cabin-only-motel that had survived since 1951.

It was a wonder that it was on the net at all, when George searched it at the vet's, being it was so antiquated. It was about fifty miles north of Seattle, off the main highway, so PC culture hadn't caught up with it yet, judging from the lobby restrooms that read, *Chiefs* and *Squaws*.

Once he got the keys, he gave one to Chang and Angela who headed off to their cabin. George and Angela waited twenty minutes in the lobby for Miles to arrive. George paced while Cathy browsed through some Zane Grey pocketbooks yellowed with age.

Finally, Mile's headlights appeared through the downpour and turned under the lobby overhang. George and Cathy went out to meet him.

Miles rolled down his window. "What's with you and this *Crazy Horse* situation?"

George didn't want to go into details. "You got the brought the money?"

"Yeah, here you go." Miles handed him the black, attaché type soft bag with the thirty-thousand dollars in it.

"I appreciate this, Miles. Did you get the food?"

"Yeah. Back seat. Enough for you and ... your tribe for a few days."

George opened the back door of the car, put the bag on top of the larger of two boxes of groceries and picked it up. Cathy grabbed the other one. "Did you get any plates and forks?" Cathy asked.

"Just what you see there. Nobody mentioned plates and utensils."

"No problem, Miles," George said. "Okay. Get back home and keep your phone on ..."

"On loud, right. But what's going on?"

"Look. You're not involved with any of this, so you can help me out when I need you, with no danger to yourself."

"Danger? What the hell, George?"

"Drive safe."

"I'm not driving anymore in this storm. I'll stay here."

"No, not here. You should stay out of this."

"All right. I'll grab a motel back in Marysville."

"That's good. You'll be closer when I need stuff."

"Hey George. I'm not your delivery boy ... But ... I'd like to stick close to that bag of cash. It's still mine, right?"

"Sure." George looked at his past competitor and then added, "You know, you're really being great about this, Miles."

"Yeah, I know."

"I'll call you in the morning."

"Right." Miles rolled up his window and drove off. George and Cathy ran in the rain and lightning to cabin six. They were half-soaked by the time George got the door open. Setting the boxes of groceries down, George flipped the light switch turning on a single dim light bulb in the ceiling fan which started spinning.

"Well," Cathy sighed out looking at antiquated room. "Any port in a storm, I guess."

"It looks like Chief Crazy Horse himself designed this," George said. Looking at the ceiling, he could see at least five places that were leaking water. One of them over the fan which was spraying water around. "I'd better get us another room. I don't feel like sleeping in a wet bed." George grabbed two towels from the bathroom, tossed one to Cathy and began drying his hair with the other one.

"You know what, George? Get a separate room for yourself. I don't feel like sleeping in any bed, wet or dry, with you."

"What? What's the matter? Why didn't you say so in the lobby?"

Cathy began drying her hair. "I've been waiting to be alone with you so we can talk."

"All right. Let's talk."

"Those people you got me involved with threatened my life. I don't know why. But I know it's your fault."

"I'm sorry it happened."

"But you did something to me, George, didn't you?"

George tossed his towel on a dusty side table. "What do you mean?"

"I've got more energy, stronger, need less sleep ... All that. Just like you."

"Oh, Jesus."

"What?" Cathy tossed her towel on top of his.

"What's 3 times 675?"

Cathy didn't hesitate. "Two-thousand-twenty-five. Why?"

George picked up a large ash tray sitting on a side table and throw it at her full. Cathy caught it with one hand. Her rage flashed and she threw it back at him. He caught it. "Jesus. I gave it to you, didn't I? Gave you ... power."

"You gave it to me, all right. Now what? Am I stuck with this thing? Is it going to eventually kill me?"

"Not as far as I know."

"As far as you know?" She blew out a breath of air and yelled, "Right, George. Right."

Now George's blood was up. "Yes," he yelled at her. "I'm not sure where this energy will lead. So, what can I say?"

Cathy yelled back louder, "You got this ... this energy when you were in San Francisco, didn't you?"

"Yes, it happened there."

Cathy took a step toward him. "What happened, exactly?"

"It's just ... There was this girl."

Now Cathy's anger boiled over, but she had enough presence of mind to snap on the large, old-style, wooden-boxed TV loud to drown out the argument that was now too loud and too intimate for other's ears.

· The channel that went on had a woman singing a blues number. It reminded George of Veronica turning on his hotel TV to an opera, to muffle her screaming, though her screaming wasn't out of anger. "Why not the opera?" he said to humor himself in this bad situation.

"Opera? You took that girl to the opera?"

"No, it's nothing."

Cathy put her hands on her hips and yelled over the singing woman. "So, you got this power from her, right? ... Sexually, I guess?"

"You've got the brain power now, so I guess you figured it out."

"You got it from screwing her. And now the both of you have screwed me, too." She took a breath nodding her head in understanding. "And I guess you didn't use a condom, so you risked my life on some hooker you met at the convention?"

"She's wasn't a hooker."

"Hooker or not, you two didn't have time to take a blood test. And you didn't take one when you came back."

"Hey, Cathy. What can I say? It just happened quickly, and it was over quickly."

"Those things just don't happen. You met her by choice, not chance. Met her at your hotel the night you blew me off the phone with 'Room service is coming. I gotta stop talking.' It came all right. Both of you came."

"Come on, stop it, Cathy. All right. I messed up. What do you want?"

"What do I want?" She screamed. "What do I want?" She lunged at George with both her hands slapping his face, and with her now enhanced power, it hurt like hell. He let the first three slaps go by and then stopped her upcoming fourth. He grabbed her around her waist, pinning her arms down.

"Stop it," he yelled.

"Make me," she challenged.

George had never seen Cathy enraged like this. He had also never seen her so empowered. He never considered that he could pass on Veronica's power to someone else, but now he was faced with it.

What does a couple do with newly acquired powers and pent up rage? George released Cathy's arms. She was always the shy one, the passive one.\ But not tonight. With the storm raging outside, Cathy was raging inside. "Make me stop," she repeated.

Was he getting the wrong signal from her as he pushed her onto the bed? Cathy's hand on the back of his head pulling him down to her lips, told George that he wasn't. With her new power, Cathy was no longer shy and passive. To the contrary.

The blues singer on TV, the rainwater splashing around them, the wind and thunder outside, and their mutual powers from within, all combined into lasciviousness for Cathy, delirium for George.

Flashes of the images that Veronica had showed him when she laid hands on his brain, came to George; the train crash in Las Vegas, the strangulation of the young man she had recruited, the inhuman hand that had reached out and victimized Veronica. *I'll take you to the next level*, she had promised George. "What's the next level?" George shouted out over the sound of the thunder and TV.

"What? What is it?" Cathy cried out.

As their rapture increased, so did the lightning and thunder outside. Rainwater leaked heavily through the roof bouncing off the bedpost, nightstand and a tabletop that had a cheap wooden bust of an Indian warrior on it. George turned his head away from Cathy momentarily and saw the warrior staring at him.

The leak above the spinning fan became heavier, making an inside rainstorm that neither George nor Cathy noticed. A loud rock band replaced the blues singer on TV turning the room into a two-person bacchanal in the middle of a tempest that Bacchus would have been proud of.

In his mind, George could see Veronica walking away from him and looking back as she had done at the convention. "Don't go. Come back," he called out, looking at Cathy on the bed under him, but seeing Veronica.

"Who are ... you talking ... to?" Cathy gasped out.

George refocused his mind, so that Cathy's face returned. "She's perfect," he breathed out, "addiction."

"Stop it, George. Get the hell out of me." But he didn't. Nor did she make him.

Was it 20 minutes or an hour later, that a rotten, wind-broke tree-limb came crashing through the cabin window? They didn't know. But the rain and wind, that now blew the dusty, white curtains over them like flying ghosts, brought a mutual-frenzied ending to their confrontation.

George got to his feet backing away from the bed, still with visions of Veronica. "What's the next level?" he yelled out with wind and rain from the broken window hitting him.

The TV now had the weather report on. "The storm that's hit Seattle and its outlining areas has caused ..." George grabbed the heavy wood-cased set, yanking the plug and cable out of their outlets and flung it across the room like a Frisbee. It crashed into the opposite wall and fell to the floor.

Cathy jumped out of the bed, her long blond hair flying in the wind and rain. She grabbed a sheet and covered herself, backing into the corner of the cabin away from George. With both their chests heaving to recover from their coupling, they stared at each other like enemy felines, wondering what their next move would be and who would move first.

Suddenly, the cabin door crashed open as Chang barged in shirtless, his pistol in both hands pointing around the room, searching for intruders. He'd been alerted from his cabin by the sound of the breaking window.

He saw George standing in one corner of the cabin naked and Cathy in the other holding the sheet over herself. Between them was the broken window and the tree branch in the middle of the room. "What the hell's going on?"

"We're practicing fighting, in case we get married," Cathy screamed out belligerently.

"What?" Chang said.

Angela entered the room from behind Chang. She quickly surveyed the situation. "We'd better get them another cabin."

"Make it two cabins," Cathy yelled over a thunder-clash. "And keep that son-of-a-bitch away from me."

CHAPTER 5

1

In his cabin, Veronica's rescuer, Don Hoffman, sat at his kitchen table with his laptop in front of him. He planned to do some work, but the beautiful stranger sleeping under a blanket on his sofa kept distracting him.

She had not spoken a word since she arrived, not even to echo him. He opted to put her on the sofa, since the nearby fireplace still had some wood burning in it. The warmth and hypnotic crackle from there did the job he had hoped for and helped put her into a deep sleep.

He was happy she didn't awaken when he removed her wet, sandy dress before gently positioning a pillow under her head and covering her with a blanket.

Now the image of her long black hair and dark, Native-American features on the white of the pillow, kept him looking.

Next to the sofa was the woman's snakeskin bag that held that horrible-faced Navajo doll. *What's the story behind that?* He wondered.

He figured that the only way he could help this amnesiac was to find some identification in her purse. But he had hesitated to do that in favor of letting her come to her senses and finding out about her naturally. But now his curiosity was peaking.

Getting up he approached the sofa and slowly reached into the bag. That damned doll looked like it was ready to bite him. But he shoved that out of his mind and found a small snakeskin-like plastic case. *She really likes the snake stuff*, he thought.

Opening the case, he found a driver's license as well as some credit cards with the name Veronica Hawthorne on them. Her license had a San Francisco address on it. *What was she doing alone on a Washington beach?*

Don replaced the cards and license and slowly, gently, closed the case. The quiet snap of the lock made Veronica sit up like an awakening zombie. Don was startled frozen. Her eyes locked on him.

Seemingly still in a trace, she pulled the blanket off her and let it drop to the floor. She lay back down on the sofa positioning herself to entice.

Was it the heat from the fireplace or from her flushed skin that he was feeling?

"She reached out her arms to him."Come."

Another man might have resisted her coaxing out of fear of involvement, health or a jealous husband. But another man hadn't been womanless for two years. Don could not take his eyes off the hypnotic beauty she was now openly displaying.

He went with it.

2

"Hungry."

Don opened his eyes and sat up in bed to see Veronica standing over him without stitch one of clothing. Once she had finished with him, or so he felt, on the sofa, he retired to his own bed.

"Okay, I'll fix something right up," he said, getting out of bed in his underwear. He slowly took the top blanket off his bed, so as not to startle her with any quick movements and draped it around her shoulders.

She instinctively took hold of the sides of the blanket and closed them over the front of her body. "Where am I?"

"It's okay. You're safe in my home." He got into a pair of jeans and a T-shirt and then walked toward the kitchen. "Come on," he said gently. "It'll be all right."

She followed. "I'm very hungry."

"Yeah," he said with a smile. "Your dress should be dry by now, but you can put on one of my sweaters and pants over there," he said, pointing to them on a chair. "Get dressed and I'll start breakfast."

She went over to the chair, dropped the blanket and slowly got into his clothes as Don fired up the stove. "Eggs, bacon and toast coming right up."

Now dressed, she sat down at the large, wooden table that served both for eating and work. "This is your home?" she asked.

"Yes," he said, putting bread in the toaster. "So, it seems like your speaking more. Are you feeling ...?

"Where is this place?"

"It's Washington ... Washington state. About fifty minutes north of Seattle." He looked at her. She seem to understand his answer. He cracked three eggs into the pan. "So ... by the way ... I'm Don Cavanaugh. I'm ... ah ... single." He covered that bit of information with a chuckle. "I work here at home doing internet sales and such." He put two strips of bacon next to the eggs.

"Internet sales and such?"

"Yes, that's right. And now according to our local custom here in this neck of the woods, after I tell you my name and occupation, you tell me yours."

Veronica jerked her head like she was trying to remember, but only asked, "Local custom?"

"Well, I was just trying my hand at being charming. But I'm a little out of practice, sorry to say. Anyway, do you feel like telling me who you are? I mean, since we've gotten ... ah, familiar with each other, at least a first name would help our conversation."

"We're having a conversation now."

"Yes, we are. So ... ah, who are you?"

"I'm ... I'm not sure." The jerkiness in her head movements had subsided some. "I don't think I know. I think I can't remember."

"Well, obviously, something happened to you out there on the beach or in the ocean," Don said keeping an eye on both her and the sizzling bacon and eggs. "Were you in the water a long time?

"I think I was."

"Well, don't worry about it. I read that amnesia never lasts long. You're just tired and maybe a little shell-shocked from whatever happened to you."

"I really need to eat."

"Yeah, right. Coming up," he said, grabbing a plate. "You know I want to keep you happy, so that you might stick around for a while. I haven't had a guest here in a long time." He put the bacon and eggs and toast on a dish. "I moved up here from Seattle ... after my divorce ... to get away from all that crowded city crap. Oh man, once my ex made me go up in the Space Needle." He shook his head to shake off the memory as the toast popped up. He grabbed it.

Veronica turned and looked at him. "Your ex?"

He served her the breakfast. "Yeah, but she's out of the picture now. Say, I don't suppose you remember if you're married or not? ... I mean, you're not wearing a ring or anything, so I was just wondering."

She picked up a fork and began to eat. "I don't think so."

"Oh, interesting," he said controlling his elation, even though her memory could not be trusted completely at this point.

Don sat down across from her and grabbed a cold cup of coffee sitting next to his computer left over from when he didn't care. He just needed something to hold. "So anyway, maybe a walk on the beach would help jog your memory. You know sometimes ..."

As Don talked, Veronica suddenly had a faint memory come to her. *A house. Where? Arizona. A face. Someone or something is waiting there.*

She started to formulate a plan. "Do you live alone here?" she asked him in a stronger voice than she had been able to muster since the beach.

"Oh, yeah. Don't worry. We're alone here. There are some other cabins in the area scattered around. But no one comes here unless I invite them."

"Good," she said not looking up from her food as she ate.

"You can stay here as long as you want. You know, rest up from whatever happened to you."

"I'd like that."

"So, about last night," Don said hesitantly.

She continued eat, so maybe his statement didn't register or qualify for an answer.

Don took a sip of cold coffee. "So, anyway. What did happen to you yesterday?"

"I died."

3

"Okay, that's the last of it," Miles said as he put down the fifth box of supplies in George's new cabin-turned-base-of-operations. "And here's the keys to the SUV."

"Have many seats?" George asked.

"It's big. They didn't have the nine. But I got the eight-passenger model."

"Good enough," George said talking the keys.

"Why all the seats?"

"Three's four of us. We just need the space."

"Got it on a weekly rental."

"Thanks, Miles

Miles looked at Chang, Angela and Cathy setting up the room with large, detailed Seattle maps, laptops, mini-cams, electronic cables and more.

"I'll call you when I need you," George told Miles.

Miles held his hands up in a '*what's going on?*' position.

"That's all for now," George said, giving Miles the bums' rush. "We have to talk about things, so let us the room, please."

"No, George," Miles said. "You've been slaving me around for the last two days with buying things for you, so I want to know what's going on. If I'm going to be an accessory to some kind of crime, I have the right to know."

"Let him stay," were the first words that Cathy said to George since the night of the storm. She had sulked in her own cabin while George and Chang planned things. Now she was ready to be involved in taking down her kidnappers. "Miles has a right to know what's going on."

George looked at Chang who shrugged a 'I guess it's okay' motion.

"All right, Miles," George said. "Come on outside and I'll explain things."

They stepped outside the cabin. George filled Miles in, purposely leaving out the part about calling and inviting Veronica to his hotel room when they were in San Francisco. Miles had asked George about her when they flew back to Seattle, but George said he hadn't called her. And of course, George left out the part about killing Veronica and having a boatman dump her body in the ironically named Possession Sound.

"Jesus," Miles injected at a few points in the story about Michaelson's group, the selling short and kidnapping of Cathy.

"So, now it's down to this," George concluded, "They will continue to build their groups and eventually take over, unless someone gets proof and alerts the right authorities."

Stepping back inside the cabin, Miles said, "I see why you had me buy all this surveillance equipment for you."

"So now," George said, "we're still debating what to do exactly."

"What about just going to the police?" Miles asked.

"Go to the police?" Angela questioned. "With a story like that?"

"I saw a senator at the party," George said, "so it's more than likely that Michaelson has already infiltrated the local and probably state police."

"Well, I gotta tell you," Miles said. "My mind is now officially boggled. Is all this really happening?"

"It's all true, Miles," Cathy said. "So, it's best to keep your distance from us."

Angela took a step forward. "You know, at our karate school, we have our students' contact information in our computer."

"So?" Chang questioned, still uncomfortable with his wife's involvement in this.

"So, maybe this guy Michaelson has a list of his people."

"It could work," George said, way ahead of her. "We hack into his computer and get all the information that we can and take it to the FBI in Washington. And I'm talking D.C., not here."

"You can't hack a guy like that," Miles said. "He's sure to have firewalls on top of firewalls." Miles folded his arms and widened his stance as he started thinking deeply.

"Okay, so we can't hack him," George said. "How about, we get into his house and download his information directly. Anything that ties him to any act of sabotage and hopefully the names of his followers."

The five went silent for a moment. Miles still had his body in a quasi-power position, in deep contemplation.

George broke the silence. "Okay, tomorrow, the girls press on to Vancouver so we can ..."

"Bullshit, 'the girls press on to Vancouver'," Angela said.

"Ditto bullshit," Cathy said.

George looked at the two women. "Or else we all go to Vancouver and forget this."

"I'm not running from any damned terrorists who shot me," Chang said. "I ran away to get you two out of the house. I ran away to get on the boat to join my wife. But that's the last of my running."

"I feel the same as you, Mr. Chang," George said. "But still, I don't know."

"You don't know, George?" Miles said loudly, stepping into the center of the room. "You don't know? What the hell? They're terrorists. George, you talked about Billy Jack before ..."

"Miles," George said. "This has nothing ..."

"Well, when in doubt," Miles continued on his roll, "ask yourself 'What would Billy Jack do?'"

George smirked knowing they all needed the levity.

"And the answer would come back," Miles continued, "Billy Jack would take his right foot and whop the man on the right side of his head. And there ain't nothin' the man can do about it."

The four of them looked at Miles incredulously.

"What the hell?" Chang said.

"Look," George said, "How this? We infiltrate one of his parties. He seems to have them on a regular basis. Lots of people there to mix in with."

"Might work," Chang said.

"Yeah," George continued, his enhanced mind seeing a plan quickly evolve. "We wire-tap his phone and when we get word of his next party, that's when we infiltrate."

"Do you know how to tap phones?" Cathy asked.

"I'm a quick study of most things these days," he said to her. "So are you, come to that."

"Ha, ha," she said, to the puzzlement of the rest of them.

"No one's going to talk about sensitive stuff on the phone," Miles offered.

"A party isn't sensitive," George countered. "Ordering food, isn't sensitive. And they'll use the phone to do that. And that's when we'll know about an upcoming party."

"It might work," Chang said.

"So, at their next party, one of us goes in there." George paused to look at Angela, "It's mostly beautiful women there and then ..."

"Whoa," interrupted Chang. "That's not the direction I thought you were going in. And that's not going to happen."

"You knew where this was going when we all decided to get off the boat together," George said.

Chang stepped closer to George. "Not her."

"They already know Cathy," George reminded Chang. "And of course, you and me. If we choose this route, then that's the only way."

"Then we don't choose this route," Chang said.

"I can get it done," Angela volunteered. "I can at least find where his computer is located. And if it's a laptop, put in a large purse and leave."

Chang gave her a look of admiration filled with fear.

"Might work," Miles said.

"No, George," Cathy said. "It's crazy to think that she ..."

"No problem," Angela said. "I go in, have a drink, flirt a little, find his computer, I'm in, I'm out, hello, good-bye. I leave with the rest of the guests with a laptop or a thumb drive full of names."

"What do you know about thumb drives?" Chang asked her.

"I know what they are. And what I don't know, I can learn here," Angela said pointing to the laptops on the desk.

"It's safe enough, I think," George said. "When I was at the party, there were lots of women. Some escorted, some not. If Angela acts like a party girl. You know, act drunk if they find her in the wrong room, it could work safely."

"I can do it," Angela said.

Chang took a deep breath. "I might go along with it, if we have a back-up team of you, me and a couple others. You know. In case something goes wrong while she's in there."

"Where are we going to get a couple of other guys?" George wanted to know.

"I'll handle that, Chang said."But first I want Angela to go there with a date as cover and back up. It makes her presence there more believable. And, whoever goes, can assist with the download, keep watch, protection, calling us for help. All that."

"Michaelson and his guards already saw you, me and Cathy," George reminded him.

"They saw Angela on the boat," Chang said.

"From far away during a gunfight, mixed you will you guys," Angela said. "They didn't get a look at my face," Besides, I'll wear a ponytail and different clothes. What's one more girl in a house full of girls?"

"Well, it should work," Chang said. Now, who goes to the party with her?" Chang asked.

The room went silent for a moment. Then Cathy's head turned. So did Chang's, followed by Angela and George.

With four sets of eyes on him, Miles started taking baby-steps backwards. "Oh, no," he said slowly while shaking his head like a death-row convict that got woken up by the warden. "No. No sir-ee Bob dixie."

"Bob dixie?" Questioned George. "What happened to Billy Jack?"

Mile's backward trek was stopped by the cabin wall. "Yeah," he smiled weakly. "One tin soldier rides away."

CHAPTER 6

1

Richard Tasserly was just entering his office where he traded stocks and managed money for his clients, when he got a call from George. He punched his cell phone. "Yeah, George. How's it going?"

"Okay, Richard. Say, what's the value of my remaining stocks?"

"Well, you cashed your biggest win with that train shorting, so you have about six-hundred thousand and some change with the others you're holding. But like I told you, no more shorting."

"That's fine, Richard. Cash it all out and put it into my bank account."

"You really want to do that?"

"I can't explain right now. Just please get it done."

"Sure. All right," Richard said, sitting down at his cluttered desk. "We're still friends, right, George?"

"Always. And don't worry, I'm out of the shorting business. Anyway, please do that for me as soon as possible."

"You got it, genius boy."

"When will it be available?"

"You can hit the bank in 24 hours."

2

The bank in the small town of Marysville didn't have all the cash George wanted, but the manager gave him enough for the upcoming needs of his group and a special bank card to access more later.

As he was exiting the bank where Miles was waiting for him in the SUV, a limousine pulled up, inadvertently blocking him. For some reason, George was curious about who was in it, so instead of walking around the limo, he waited.

A young, tall handsome Native American man in an expensive suit got out. He reached in to help an elderly Native American man out of the limo who was equally well-dressed. The younger man reached into the limo and grabbed an alligator-skin briefcase. He took the old man's arm and they slowly proceeded toward the bank door.

When the old man saw George, he stopped and turned toward him. For a moment, their eyes were locked on each other. The old native with his turquoise necklace, headband and weathered face made an impressive sight to George, who figured the man must be over ninety.

The old man gently pushed the younger man's helping arm aside and turned and started to slowly walk toward George. The younger man waited and watched like the bodyguard he seemed to be. The old man approached George while looking deep into his eyes as if searching for something there.

George stood still, echoing the fascination this man seemed to have for him. The man placed his hands on George's shoulders. With what seemed to be a knowing smile, the man said something in his native language. Maybe ten or fifteen words.

The man then patted the right side of George's face, nodded, and turned back to his bodyguard, taking his arm. The two slowly walked into the bank.

George made his way over to where Miles was parked sitting behind the wheel. He rolled down the window. "What was that all about?"

"I'm not sure?"

"It looked like the two of you were sharing a moment."

"Yeah, I know we were. But what kind of moment, I have no idea."

3

In his cabin, Don was working at his computer when he felt Veronica approaching from behind, after awakening from her nap. He was the happiest he'd been in years, because she had accepted his invitation to share his bed for the rest of her stay. A stay that he hoped would never end.

He felt the warmth of her hands on the back of his neck. "All caught up on your sleep?" he asked.

"Yes, I think so. She moved over to the chair next to him and sat down."It's nice here."

"I'm glad you're comfortable. And I'm glad that you're able to talk more. I think you're eventually going to get completely well, if take your time, relax and let yourself get stronger."

"Do you ever go out?"

"Sure. A couple times a week. Groceries and stuff. But I'm pretty much self-contained."

"I see."

"I do my work online here. Get paid online. I do live video meetings on this as well, wearing a coat and tie while sitting here in my shorts." He smiled at her.

Veronica made no response, as humor hadn't returned to her yet. And what little humor she had in the past, was only used to entice and control people. "I remember my home."

He stopped typing and turned to face her, trying not to show his disappointment, because the more she remembered the sooner she might leave. "Oh? .... Well, ... that's good." He hated to ask her, but he had to. "Where do you live?"

"I have an apartment in San Francisco, but my hometown is in Arizona."

"Arizona, huh? Then why ...?

"Winslow."

"Then why were you on the beach like that?"

"I don't remember," she said. The mental faculties that were quickly returning to Veronica, now included her innate ability to lie undetected. "You have a car outside," she said as a statement, not a question.

"Sure. But I don't think you'd ..."

"Drive me there."

"San Francisco?"

"Winslow."

He was perplexed and had to think fast. "Are you sure you want to go there?"

"Yes."

"When?"

"Now."

"Ah, well," Don said, trying to decide whether to go with her or send her on her way. Separation at this point would be too painful to endure, so he said, "I guess the two of us going there is possible."

"Good."

"But not today."

Disappointment came to her face.

"But in two days. How about two days? Okay?"

"How long is the drive?"

"Ah, I don't think by car, though. Flying is better." Now Don decided to sneak in the big one, now that her memory seemed complete. She was not sure before when he asked her about being married or not. Now Don wanted to be sure, before he got in deeper than he already was. "Can your husband meet you at the airport?"

"I'm not married."

Bingo, he thought, but needed one more. "Don't you have a boyfriend that can meet you there?"

"I have no one on earth."

Don smiled. "That makes two of us."

She forced a smile to match his, but only out of manipulation.

"And that," Don said, reaching in and kissing her check, "makes us an intriguing couple."

"Intriguing?"

He cupped her face in his hands. "Very special."

"You have no idea."

He leaned back and turned to his computer. "Well. Let's see. Winslow, Arizona, huh?" He brought up an Arizona map on his screen. "I'll tell you what. I'll book us a flight to Flagstaff," he typed 'United Airlines'into his browser. "And then we'll rent a car and drive to Winslow."

"When?"

"Two days. A day and a half from now. Just so I can take care of a few things."

"Okay. A day and a half."

"What do you plan to do when we get there?"

"Dig for gold and jewelry."

He turned toward her again and smiled "A very fine plan. Sounds like fun."

"You have no idea."

CHAPTER 7

1

"Are you finding everything you need, sir?" the overweight grocer munching on an apple asked.

"Almost. Just a few more things," Chang replied. "You got batteries here?"

"On the back wall. Right side."

"They're over here," Angela called from the back of the room.

Chang and Angela had taken the SUV to a small country-style store in the woods outside of Marysville to get groceries and a few other items. It was the first time the two of them had been away from the group in the last week of just hanging around the cabins monitoring Michaelson's phone. So, this store-run was a needed short vacation for them.

"Do we have what you need?" the grocer called back to them.

"Yeah," Chang said. "I think so."

Sometimes, hanging around just to get 'a few more things' pulls too much exposure for someone that is trying to stay under the radar. The exposure came with the sound of three motorcycles coming to a stop outside the store. Chang heard them, but even with his street smarts, he didn't think the street would show up at this out of the way place.

This time, the street came in the form of three, thirsty bikers who, when seeing the new SUV, took an instant liking to it. They thought it would be nice to sleep in at the end of a day's ride. Of course, they never thought to buy one, when commandeering one would be much easier, and cheaper.

From the back of the store, Chang heard the rattling sound of spurs on the wooden store floor. A large, bearded biker entered purposely walking heavy-footed to make his spurs announce him. He was the leader of the two bikers that followed him, by virtue of seniority, his size, and innate hostility.

Chang looked over and could see them down the aisle getting beers out of the refrigerator. He knew that bikers could cause trouble just out pure malevolence. So, he figured that it was time to pay the bill, grab the goods and get him and Angela back to their cabins. Chang started heading toward the counter.

"What about the batteries?" Angela asked quietly.

"Forget them," he whispered. "I'll get some later."

As he and Angela approached the counter, Chang took a quick glance at the three men. He noticed the .45 automatic tucked in the leader's belt. "What this all come to?" Chang asked the grocer.

"Well, if that's it for you, then it's $275.37. Call it two-seventy-five."

Chang knew the bikers would eye whatever cash he pulled out, so he reached into his pocket and with his fingers felt out three of the hundred dollar bills that George had given him. He pulled them out and handed them to the grocer. "Keep it."

"Oh, thank you, sir. Much appreciated."

Before Chang and Angela could grab the boxes, the biker leader said, "I like that car of yours."

"Yeah, it's nice," Chang replied quietly without looking at them.

Angela was hoping Chang would end his reply there, but she knew her husband.

"It's an SUV," Chang continued. "Dealers have them in stock if you want one."

The other two bikers moved up next to their leader to form a wall on the way leading to the door. The leader gave Chang a look of distain, and then said, "I didn't say, I'd like a car *like that*. I said, I like *your* car, Charlie Chan."

Angela took a deep breath knowing what was to come. She'd seen it before, once when she first met and was rescued by Chang. And another time when two drunks at a restaurant got out of line. She had half a mind to say a prayer for these three degenerates.

"And we like your daughter, too," the bull-necked biker on the leader's left added.

Chang finally turned his head toward them in what comedians would call the '*slowly I turned*' moment. But an ex-con like Chang would never consider the '*step by step, inch by inch*' part of it. When he attacked, it was always by surprise. "She's my wife," he said, sizing up the three, like he sized up convicts in the prison yard.

"Your wife?" the leader said, genuinely surprised. "Well, more power to you, old man."

Now, Angela forgot about the prayer for them. She wanted to see them in pain. She was from the streets, too. And she never liked loud-mouth-pushy-milquetoast men that used weapons, cars and bikes as substitutes for their dicks. She was funny that way.

"You know," the leader said, eye-screwing Angela, and then looking down at her legs that the shorts she was wearing revealed. "I wouldn't mind having those outstanding legs wrapped around me. She seems like a real sex-biscuit."

Now, Angela wished Chang piled all the pain he could muster on them. Then, when Chang took a step back from the counter, she could see the leader's belt and the .45 he had in it. Now a prayer did come to her mind, but now it was for Chang and her to get out of there unharmed.

Chang took a few steps to place himself in front of the three men. "You know," he said calmly. "It's very childish and rude to remark on a woman's sexually like that. I could make remarks about you and your friends' sexuality, but I won't."

"Oh? You wouldn't?" the leader smirked.

"No," Chang said softly. He looked at the biker on the right. "For example, I wouldn't call him *limp dick*." He looked to the man on the left, "or him *tiny balls*." He looked dead into the leader's eyes. "And I wouldn't call you *numb nuts*."

The leader's right hand began to creep to his pistol.

"Don't try it. I've stomped on guys bigger than you in three different prisons."

"Well that's the difference between me and you. I never let *the man* put me in prison, or even jail." He quickly grabbed his pistol and pulled it out.

Faster than Angela could follow, Chang, using a two-handed aikido technique, ripped the pistol away from the biker and aimed it at him. All three bikers froze with baffled expressions. "Hey, man. Cool it," the leader slowly said as he stared into the barrel of his own pistol. "I was only fooling around. Give me back my pistol please."

"You've never seen it from this end, I bet," Chang said.

"Come on, man. What do you want?"

Chang quickly pulled back the slide of the pistol making the biker flinch and yell out, "Oh, my god."

Angela blinked as she thought Chang was going to fire the pistol into the biker's face.

A bullet popped out pistol which Chang caught with one hand. Chang slowly brought the bullet up to the biker's face. "Eat it."

The leader turned to look at the biker on his right who was bedazzled by what just happened. He had never seen his leader disarmed, nor as perplexed.

"Come on," Chang hissed out. "Eat it."

The leader's face slowly changed from fear to 'don't give a shit' outrage. He made a sudden grab for the pistol. Chang instantly swatted down the biker's hand and with his same hand back-fisted the biker in the bridge of the nose making him scream. He followed that with a straight punch to the jaw, making the biker's head band fly across the store, followed by the biker who landed in a shelf of canned goods.

Chang tossed the gun to Angela who pointed it at the ground for safety. Figuring that a woman wouldn't shoot them, the two bikers sprang into action, attacking Chang.

Most women would have averted their eyes from her husband's bone smashing rampage and covered her ears from the screams of pain coming from his adversaries. But most women hadn't been victimized by animals like this in their past. The final agonizing howl from the leader on the floor with the heel of Chang's boot in his groin almost brought Angela to euphoria.

But while watching the three bikers squirm on the floor in pain, she caught hold of herself. Moving back to the reality of the situation, her euphoria quickly turned to anger. It was Chang who couldn't just ignore the insults and just walk out with the groceries. Chang who endangered their lives by going against a gun carrying biker.

And they still weren't out this, yet. What if the grocer called the police? It wouldn't go very well with her husband being an ex-con who was incarcerated for manslaughter twelve years ago. *What an asshole he is*, she thought.

Chang walked over to her, his face still flushed from anger. Or was it excitement, she wondered. He looked at the grocer to make sure he wasn't reaching for any phone, but the man was standing there frozen with his hands in the air. Chang handed Angela the keys to the SUV. "Get in and start it up."

"What are you going to do?"

"Carry out the groceries and make sure none of these badasses don't get up to follow."

She gave him an angry look and headed for the door, pistol in hand at her side. "What's your problem?" he asked to her back.

"You're the one with the problem," she said without turning around.

Chang pulled out another hundred from his pocket and tossed it on the counter in front of the terrified grocer. "Don't call anybody. Right?"

The grocer scooped up the bill. "Right, sir."

Chang stacked one box on top of the other and grabbed the bottom one. With his blood still up from bone-breaking, the full boxes felt light in his arms.

Angela had wiped clean the pistol, threw it into some bushes, opened the side door of the SUV and was sitting behind the wheel with the motor running as Chang arrived. He put the boxes on the floor behind the front seat. "Close the door," he said to Angela who hit the button. He turned and started walking back to the store.

"Hey. Where are you going?"

"The team needs batteries."

Now she was really pissed off. They could get batteries anywhere. But obviously Chang wanted to gloat over his fallen enemies a little longer. *What a jackass*, she thought.

The grocer was surprised to see Chang coming back and immediately raised his hands again. On the way to the battery rack, amidst the groans and cries of pain coming from the floor, Chang had to step over the biker leader. He was still writhing in pain, his silver spurs making a happy jingle powered by his shuttering legs. He saw Chang pass above him and cried out, "You broke my god-damned arm, you son-of-a-bitch."

Chang grabbed five packs of double A batteries off the rack, walked back to the grocer and tossed them on the counter.

"Oh, no, no," the grocer said. "Your tip covered them. They're yours."

"Thank you," Chang said picking them up. "You could get our license plate and call this in. But I wouldn't advise it because if you do, I'll come back and raise hell."

"Don't worry, mister. No phone calls."

"When these crybabies catch their breath, give 'em a beer and let them leave."

"Sure thing."

"Thank you." Chang headed to the door.

One of the fallen bikers reached out from the floor and grabbed Chang's leg. Chang's ended his grip by stomping on his wrist. His high-pitched, little-girl's scream was music to Chang's ears. "Now stay down there and keep your asshole friends down for the next ten minutes or I'll come back and break your other wrist."

Still screaming, the biker couldn't acknowledge Chang's request. But Chang figured he got the message and continued out the door with the needed batteries in hand.

He jumped into the passenger seat of the SUV, closed the door and tossed the batteries in one of the boxes behind him.

"Okay," Angela said in a huff. "Now if Charles Bronson is finished with his shopping, can we please get out of here?"

Chang gave her a look and then glanced at her bare legs. *Perfect and beautiful, yes. But what the hell?* "Why do you dress like that?" he groaned.

"What are you talking about. This is a blouse and shorts."

"That's what I'm talking about."

"You never complained about it before."

"Let's go, will you?"

She angrily jerked the SUV into *drive* and pulled away from the store. "And what about you? You just had to show them, didn't you?" "Damn. You can take the man out of prison, but you can't take the convict out of ...

"They were asking for it. That guy drew his gun."

"Don't tell me. Go tell your students that excuse. You told them you can always defuse a situation." She pulled onto the one lane forest road that lead back to the cabins.

"Defuse, my ass. I loved beating the crap out of those pricks."

"Now the truth comes out."

"You're damned right. That's my truth."

"Jesus, my hands are shaking on the wheel," she said. "I need a drink. Did you remember to get my root beer?"

Still pissed off he answered. "Yeah, I got a six-pack." He turned back to the boxes of groceries and started rummaging around.

"Don't break the boxes."

"Don't worry about it." He pulled out a root of beer. "I've got one. It's warm."

"I don't care. Pop it open, will you?"

Chang tried to twist the cap off, but it was not a *twisty* and couldn't do it with his large knuckled hands.

"Jesus," she said, grabbing the bottle from him and hitting the bottle top perfectly on the dashboard so that the cap popped off.

Chang, angry at her, the bikers and the overall situation, made a fist and pounded on the dashboard three times.

The door of George's cabin slammed open, startling George, Cathy and Miles. Chang entered carrying the two boxes of groceries, followed by the now cooled-off Angela. But Chang was not cooled-off at all.

"Did you get the batteries?" George asked.

Chang slammed down the boxes on the table. "Yeah, I got the damned batteries."

George watched Chang go to the sofa and sit down. "What's wrong?"

"Don't worry about it," Angela said, "He's just upset that I didn't give him his fair share of my root beer."

"What?" George asked.

Hearing that, Cathy went to the boxes of groceries and looked in.

"It's okay," Angela said. "He'll get over it."

Miles looked on in confusion as George turned to the boxes to search for the batteries.

Angela sat down next to Chang. "Hey, it's all forgotten," she told him. "What do you say we get back to it, huh?"

"Here you go," Cathy said to Chang, handing him a bottle of root beer.

He hesitated, but then grabbed it out of her hand. "Thank you." He tried to twist off the top, but again couldn't do it. Angela took the bottle from him gently, hit it on the edge of the coffee table in front of them, and handed the opened bottle to him.

Chang looked at her sweet face and then took a short drink. "This stuff of yours isn't bad."

"Even warm?"

"It's good."

She nodded.

"You know, from here on, things are gonna get hairy."

"I knew that when I got off the boat," she said.

"So, before we get back to it, and hopefully end up in Canada," Chang said, "I want to say good-bye to my sister Emma."

"Sister? That's a relative you never mentioned."

"Yeah. A sister and a brother. Such as they are. I haven't seen them or my parents since I got out of the joint."

"That's almost two years now. I know why you haven't seen your parents, but why not your sister?"

"She wouldn't understand me being an ex-con. She use to be wild like me and my brother, but she's probably settled down by now."

CHAPTER 8

1

"Throw those assholes out of her," the middle-aged, slim Asian woman yelled to the bouncer over the ear-shattering music.

"Right, boss," Baxter said to Emma.

Big Bad Baxter, as they called him, grabbed the two fighting drunks by their collars and bounced them out the doors just as Chang entered.

The crowed, noisy room was trying to look like a Vegas lounge and shake off its old dive-bar image but failing. He hadn't seen his sister Emma, since she was twenty-six, so now she'd be around forty.

Emma saw him first. "What the hell?" She said to herself, then waved and called to him. "Hey, big brother. Over here."

Baxter came back from the outside and saw Chang walking toward Emma. He quickly walked over to Chang and was about to grab his shoulder when Emma waved him off and said. "He's cool." So, Baxter went back to his spot near the door.

"So, when did you get out?"

"It's been a while, I'm afraid," Chang said.

She pointed to two open chairs by a table. "And you didn't come to see me sooner?" They sat down.

"I guess I had to figure things out, open a business and ...," he shrugged, "well, you know."

Tired of having to raise her voice, she turned toward the bar. "Hey, turn that crap down."

The bartender reached over to the amplifier behind the bar and hit the switch.

"I said, *down*, not *off*, stupid."

He turned it back on and kept it low.

"Are you all right now?" she asked. "I mean no more trouble with the cops?"

"I've got a regular life now. I opened a dojo, got married and have ..."

"Married? Not Chinese, I guess?"

60

"She is."

"That's good. For a guy like you, that's good."

A petite, blond woman came to their table. "Get you anything?"

"Yeah, Donna," Emma said. "A beer for me." She looked at Chang. He nodded. "Two beers."

"You got it," Donna said.

Emma smiled at Chang. "So, you figured I'd still be here, huh?"

"I would have found you one way or another."

"Have you seen the folks?"

"Nah, I haven't gotten around to that, yet. I figured I'd start with you."

"Using me for a warmup, huh?"

"Yeah, I guess so. But I did really want to see you."

"Well, that's nice. I'm glad you stopped by."

"So how are things going for you these days."

"Really good. As you can see, I'm not a waitress anymore. I'm one-third owner," Emma said proudly. "Another few months, half-owner. By the end of the year, I'll own the whole damned place myself."

"How are you doing that? A rich boyfriend?"

Emma shook her head and waved a hand at him. "Oh. I've got a lot of boyfriends. And I leave them where I find them. But I'm with a gang that have really made a difference in my life this year."

Chang leaned in toward her. "What? I told you when you were a kid to stay away from those Chinatown gangbangers. They're the ones that got me the ten years inside. They're nothing but a bunch of ..."

"It's nothing like that. They're not a Chinatown gang. It's a group of real smart people," she said getting excited. "You've got to meet them. They really know what they're doing in the business world. And they help everyone who joins them. Men, women, ethnics, they don't care. And best of all, they've got some insider stock trading going for them. I don't know how they do it, but every stock tip I got from them, I've made money on. Good money."

Chang leaned back from her excitement, guessing where she was going with this.

"In fact," she continued, "I can put in a good word for you and get you an interview."

"Just where is this *group of people*?"

"They're right here in Seattle. Some white guy in this big-ass house is running the Seattle branch," Emma said at a fever-pitch. "But the real one with her hands on the controls, is an Indian chick who started with nothing. You , an American Indian. And now, I hear, she's got over three hundred businesspeople working for her. And she's gonna make me and

61

all of us super rich. I'm talking big houses, cars, servants and having some class. Real class. And that's as sure as a goose can shit."

Chang reached over and slapped her hard in the face knocking her half-off her chair.

She put her hand on her stinging cheek. "What the hell was that for?"

Seeing this, Baxter rushed over to Emma's aid. He grabbed Chang by the jacket, but in a flash and twist of the wrist, Baxter fell to his knees with his grimacing face hitting the table.

"I'm going to tell you this once," Chang said standing while keeping a tight grip on Baxter's wrist. "Stay away from those people. Don't go back to that house. Get in a car or a plane and get out of town for the next month. Do you hear me? Get the hell out of town." Chang punctuated his words by slamming his fist into Baxter's face, knocking him down to the beer-stained floor.

Chang turned to the door, took a few steps, and turned around to face Emma again. "You always did stupid things. Be smart now and leave town."

Baxter, getting control of his pain, got up and ran full speed at Chang who kicked over a table in front of him. Baxter's running legs crash into it, making him do a half-flip forward and landing him on his shoulder which snapped making him scream.

The people in front of the exit, who were being entertained by all this, parted like the Red Sea as Chang approached and then regrouped as Chang left.

Emma, in order to drown out Big Bad Baxter's screaming, yelled to the bartender, "Turn it back up."

2

Veronica and Don were sitting on a United Airlines plane heading for Flagstaff, Arizona. They were an hour into their two-hour forty-minute flight and Don hadn't stopped talking since they took off.

"You know," he said to her in a low voice. "I'm not much for flying or heights in general, but since we're together now, I'll do anything to help you." He looked at her.

Veronica looked straight ahead clutching the bag that held her Navajo doll. She now remembered that she had fantasized her doll had her father's spirit in it. And that he could see all the places she took him to.

The doll also serves another more important function, she thought. *What was it?*

"I've been living alone for a couple of years now," Don continued into her right ear. "I haven't been with anyone since my divorce and then you show up out of the ocean like Venus rising from the sea or something."

She turned her head slightly as to not take the full force of his horseshit directly into her ear.

"And now," he said, "here I am up in the air ... In more ways than one. You know, it's like ..."

"Stop talking."

Don responded just like any guy, who couldn't wait to get into bed with his girl again. He obeyed.

She acknowledged his quick compliance with a nod.

Don shrugged off her disinterest and reached for a magazine. The cover had some smiling, blond, female celebrity on it that he didn't know. She looked like she was staring at him with bright, happy blue eyes. But now, Don had no interest in blonds, blue eyes or a happy demeanor in a woman. He was now hooked on dark features, willfully mysterious and controlling.

Veronica heard another sound. It was a sound that Don's voice had been drowning out for the whole flight it. It was a little girl on the seat to the right-front of her. She was talking to the doll she was holding.

The doll, Veronica thought. *I must always have my doll with me. But why?* She looked out the window. Seeing the clouds pass by under her. She thought, *wind. Wind and sand.*

Nine-year-old Chumana was awakened by the sound of the wind and sand hitting the window near her bed. She was used to the desert wind storms. But this was different. Coming through her window was an ambient green light that was getting brighter, accompanied by an oscillating hum that was getting louder. Chumana knew it had to be a visit from her mentor.

She got up and went into the living room to see her parents looking out the window. The light and vibration were intensifying.

Chumana's mother was the first to turn and see her. The terror that she saw on her mother's face, seemed comical to her. "There's nothing to worry about," Chumana said.

Neddy ran over to her, knelt down and wrapped her arms around her. "It's *Matchi Manatou* come to take us," she cried.

Chumana patted Neddy's head. "It's just my friend."

But with loud sound coming from outside mixed with her fear, Neddy didn't discern her daughter's words. "Your father's been bad his whole life. So now the evil one has come to punish us all."

Jackson turned from the window. "Nobody's gonna punish me." He reached for his double-barreled shotgun leaning on the wall. "Anyone comes through that door gets blasted."

He reached into the leather bag next to it that held his stash of whiskey and shotgun shells. He came out with a handful of double-aught-bucks. "Nobody can survive a load of this shit," he said, trying to convince himself. "I don't care if it's *Matchi Manatou* or J.C. himself coming in here. I'll spread 'em out like a crazy squaw's blanket."

Jackson got into his '*don't mess with me*' stance, that intimidated white boys who mocked his drunkenness in town. He pointed his 12-guage at the door.

"It's no good, Jackson," Neddy screamed. "You can't stop *Matchi Manatou.*"

"Bullshit," Jackson yelled, keeping his eye and weapon on the door. "This'll knock down a charging buffalo at full gallop."

Then, the rotted wooden front door began to creak and moan and expand toward them. Something, stronger than human, was pushing it front the outside. Something that didn't believe in doorknobs or invitations.

Jackson turned to Neddy holding Chumana. "Out the back."

As Jackson ran to the back door, Neddy stood up, grabbed the reluctant Chumana's hand and pulled her out the back following him. The three of them ran across the back yard and entered the wooden barn. Jackson slammed the door shut and then looked out of the of the broken window that faced his house.

In the white light that now seemed to have the intensity of the sun, he saw a human-shaped, seven-foot, green-skin creature coming out the backdoor of his house. Then he saw Charlie coming out of his shack, grabbing a pitchfork and running at the figure.

"Don't, Charlie," Koko screamed coming out of the shack, holding her two-year old child in her arms. "Come back."

Before Charlie's pitchfork could strike its target, the creature turned on him, pointed a green crystal-looking stick at him and, in a flash of green light, Charlie ceased to exist. Koko screamed and ran back into her shack to protect her child.

As the terrifying creature approached the barn, Jackson stuck his double-barrels out the broken part of the window. He was ready to pull both triggers at once, but the creature turned its attention on him. The horrible-looking face froze his action. *It is Matchi Manatou*, he thought. Not wanting Charlie's fate, Jackson let go of the shotgun, letting it fall to the floor.

This time, this door didn't breathe. It flew open. Jackson didn't move. Neddy's high-pitched scream competed with the continuous humming from outside. She let go of Chumana, ran to the far corner of the barn and hid behind a tool cabinet. She waited for death at the hands the great spirit.

What Jackson saw that night, eventually drove him mad a year later, forcing Chumana to become a ward of the state. Jackson saw the intruder walk over to Chumana on green muscular legs, stop in front of her and open its long, three-fingered hand. In it, Jackson could just make out a green, glowing crystal that seemed alive. He watched his daughter confidently reach out and take it.

Jackson eyed the shotgun on the floor but didn't have the nerve to make another try. Later, he would use it to blast away a few people and then get shot by an Arizona Marshal.

The creature, his mission seemingly accomplished, turned and left without so much as a look at Jackson or the still screaming Neddy.

In less than a minute, the loud, oscillating hum and the intense green light diminished until, in a few seconds, it was gone completely.

Jackson, Neddy and Chumana came slowly out of the barn to find Koko holding her child and crying over a pile of ashes.

4

"Folks, we've begun our decent into Flagstaff, where the current weather is a beautiful 76 degrees," the pilot informed the passengers bringing Veronica back to the present.

Don put back the magazine that he'd been reading. Unrealized by him, he hadn't found the need to put on his reading glasses. The words were clear, so he just read. "Do you mind if I say something now?" he asked Veronica.

"You seem determined to," she said pulling her doll out of its bag and holding in next to her. "Go ahead."

"I was just going to say, I've got a car already reserved for us at the airport, so we'll be on our way pretty quick."

"Good," she responded moving her fingers under the doll's blanket and shirt. She could feel the crystal.

CHAPTER 9

1

"Alright. You're all set. Just push the button on the steering wheel after you get into the mall as deep as you can. You'll have eight seconds to jump from the car and run."

"Eight seconds?" Frank questioned, like in a nightmare he couldn't wake up from. He had been brought into Michaelson's group a few months ago by a woman who approached him at a bar. Thinking he was attracting her on his own merits, he never considered he was being recruited by a terrorist group.

The sexual contact Frank had with the woman had given him enhanced mental and physical powers that he made quick use of to seduce more women. The financial benefits came soon as well, with shorting stocks that Michaelson tipped the group about.

Michaelson had told the group the story of some little girl that got empowered out in Arizona, but Frank didn't believe it. He figured the power he and the group acquired was some drug they had ingested at the parties via food or drink.

And then, bad things started happening. Like he told that guy George at a bar, "*They give you women, money, and then they make you do things. Bad things.*" When George asked him what he was going to do, Frank replied hopelessly, "*What I'm told.*"

However, now sitting in a car loaded with explosives, doing *what he was told* had gone beyond the limits of the unspeakable things he was forced to do in the past.

"Eight seconds is longer than you think," Veretti assured him. "You'll have plenty of time to run for cover. Just remember to hit the button before you jump."

Lyedecker, Michaelson's number two bodyguard after Elaine, pulled Veretti aside and whispered, "What if he chickens out and doesn't hit the button?"

"It doesn't matter," Veretti grinned. "We've got a guy to radio-trigger it."

"Good thinking," Leydecker said. "Tyler Enterprises will really take a stock dive on this one."

Veretti smirked. "That's nothing to me. I just like to watch my bombs explode and the people running."

Veretti remembered delivering the bomb to Las Vegas and wishing Michaelson had let him stay there a few days to watch the results. Better to see those things live and in person, than replayed on the news. But Veretti always followed orders, so he returned to Seattle before the bomb derailed the train. Of course, as always, Veretti recorded it off the news to show women as a seduction aid.

"Hey, what the hell are you doing," Lyedecker said, as Frank turned off the car and got out.

"I can't do this," Frank whined. "You guys made me do too many things."

"Get back in the damned car, you whimp," Lyedecker yelled grabbing Frank by the collar and shaking him.

Frank hung and shook his head. "This is the end. You can kill me, but I'm not doing this."

"Oh, yeah," Veretti said, reaching around Lyedecker to grab Frank by the throat. "We can do that and leave you right here."

Frank began to giggle hysterically as Veretti held onto him "Then just do it, you son-of-a-bitch."

Lyedecker knew what Veretti was capable of doing to Frank and was on the verge of doing it. He also knew that Michaelson wanted this job done and Frank was needed to get it done. So, to defuse the situation, and protect Frank, he turned to Veretti and said, "Let's take him back to the house for now and let Mr. Michaelson handle this."

Veretti thought for a moment, and then released his grip on Frank. "Mr. M is not going to like this."

"Phone ahead and tell him what the situation is. I know he has a backup plan for this mall gig."

"Right," Veretti said. "Yeah, his backup plan."

"Let's all get a drink before we go back, to give Mr. Michaelson some time to think."

"What are you talking about, get a drink?" Veretti asked.

"Just to kill a little time."

"Sure. I get it."

"You drive the bomb car," Lyedecker told him, ignoring his question. "Frank can ride with me."

"I'm not driving any bomb car."

"Just put the safety on and let's go," Lyedecker demanded of his subordinate.

"One of these days, Lyedecker," Veretti said, going to the trunk of the car and opening it.

"Yeah, yeah," Lyedecker gave him. "Keep playing with yourself until 'one of these days'."

Veretti punched a seven-digit deactivation code into the triggering device that ran to a blasting cap connected to six pounds of plastic explosives. He closed the truck. "Happy?" he asked Lyedecker.

"Extremely," Lyedecker said. "The Boxcar Ale House is just a mile from here."

"Right," Veretti said getting into the bomb car.

"You game, Frank?" Veretti asked.

"Yeah, I guess," Frank said, adjusting his ripped shirt as best he could. "I could use a drink. But that's not going to change my mind."

"Fine," Lyedecker said. "Hop in."

Veretti turned on the bomb car engine. Even though the bomb was disarmed for now, he kept his hand away from the red button that he had attached to the right side of the steering wheel. He looked at it for a moment, knowing his phone call to Michaelson would make sure that Frank would push it. He reached for his phone.

2

It was almost two hours later when Lyedecker and Veretti brought Frank back to Michaelson's house. The two bodyguards were only slightly buzzed off of one beer each. They knew enough not to get drunk on the job. But Frank's two and a half beers had made his very uninhibited and even more unfettered to speak his mind.

The two men brought Frank to Michaelson's library with floor to ceiling shelves overloaded with books on business, success and personal power. They sat Frank down on a plush leather chair.

"It's no use," he told the two Michaelson operatives, "You can't make me do anything anymore. So how do you like that?"

Though he said it, Frank didn't believe deep down. He know he was lost. He should have seen it coming, but it was a gradual descent. Michaelson knew well how to seduce and manipulate his male workers in increments. Bigger and bigger money, hotter and hotter women, nastier and nastier jobs, until finally, they tell you to do something like blow up a shopping mall. That's when you realize that the money and women were just stepping-stones down to everlasting agony.

While Frank waited, the house chief of security, Elaine, was in Michaelson's downstairs office, listening to an Asian woman tell her what she called 'a possible problem'.

"Anyway," the woman continued, "I'm not sure what he meant by that or if he knows anything. But I thought I should report it to you."

Elaine put her hand on the woman's shoulder. "You did the right thing to tell me." She looked the attractive woman up and down. "And how do you know this man?"

"He's my brother," Emma answered.

"Your brother?"

"I hadn't seen him in years and then he showed up at my bar. All I can tell you is that when I hinted about a group that can help people, he slapped me hard and told me to stay away."

Elaine gently moved her hand from Emma's shoulder to the back of her neck. "You mentioned our group?"

Emma knew it was back peddling time. "No, not at all," she said trying not to shutter. "I just said 'a group'. You know, like a pyramid sales group or something."

Elaine moved her face close to Emma's. "You know I could punish you for that slip of the tongue."

70

Emma felt Elaine's threat was mixed with seduction. "If I deserve it."

Elaine gave a smile that a perverted executioner might give a dead-woman-walking. "Don't worry. I'll go lightly on you."

"I'd appreciate that," Emma said, and then added the secret signal between women of their bent. "*Whatever's needed.*"

"Fine." Elaine let go of her neck."Go upstairs to the living room and wait for me there."

Emma nodded. She turned toward the stairs. "Thank you, ma'am," she said, looking back at Elaine's smile as she ascended.

When she was out of sight, Elaine gave a giggle and flopped down into Michaelson's oversized leather chair. But her moment of playing 'queen of the house' was short lived as she heard heavy footsteps coming down the mahogany stairs. She knew those footsteps well and sprang to her feet before Michaelson came to the bottom, turned down the hallway and entered his office. "Who was that?" he asked her.

"The one going upstairs?"

"Yes."

"She has some information that might be useful to us," Elaine said in her most subservient tone, that she only used with Michaelson. "I'll question her further."

"Yes, I know how you question," Michaelson said, going around his desk and sitting down. "Have fun. But not just yet. We've got a visitor coming down here in a moment."

"Anything I should know about?"

"Just a woman that you might find interesting."

Elaine smiled. "Sounds intriguing."

"Yeah, she's right up your alley. Young, pretty, naïve, and scared as hell."

"You can sure pick 'em for me, Mr. M."

"However, in this case she was chosen to help us with business."

"Either way," Elaine said, "it sounds tasty."

They heard footsteps descending. "Here she comes now," Michaelson said.

Two more of Michaelson's operatives, Hobbs and Costa, pushed a young, brown-haired woman into the office. Her tear-stained faced had a red mark on the right side of her face. It had been put there by Hobbs when she resisted being taken out of her apartment. She had no idea who these men where or where she was as she had a bag put over her head during transport. They had just now taken it off so she could get down the stairs.

"Well, well. What have we here?" Elaine said.

Michaelson looked the woman over. Then looked at his two men. "Did you guys work her over?"

"No," Costa volunteered. Then changed to, "Well, maybe a little bit 'cause she put up a hell of a fight. I'll give her that."

Michaelson stood up from this desk. "Well, you got her here in short order. That's the main thing."

"What's going on?" the woman cried. "What did I do?"

"You didn't do anything, my dear. This way, please," Michaelson said, leading the group out of his office and down a long hall. "In fact, you can do something for us."

"What do you mean?"

"You'll see," Michaelson said, stopping in front of a large double-doored room. He paused and looked at the woman. "I want to show you something very special."

The woman could hear slow, bass-pounding music coming from the other side that seemed to vibrate the doors. Michaelson pushed one door open. He grabbed her by the front of her blouse and pulled her in with him. Elaine, Costa and Hobbs followed with anticipation smirks on their lips.

When the woman saw the dark, misty room full of unclad people, she shut her eyes and tilted her head down. But the sounds of arrogant demands and the consensual obedience, coming from the group, pierced her unadulterated ears.

Michaelson, standing close behind her, grabbed the sides of her head forcing it up. "Take a long look and remember it."

Elaine stepped forward and looked at the woman. "She's got her eyes closed."

"Open them," Michaelson demanded.

Elaine punched the woman in the stomach forcing the woman's eyes to slam open and her mouth to gasp for air.

"She's looking now, boss," Elaine smiled and then turned her attention back to the room.

"Yes, keep looking," Michaelson told the woman. "Burn it all into your mind.

The woman, still grasping for air and not wanting any more of what Elaine had to offer, looked with purposefully unfocused eyes. The blurs of undulating flesh, coupled with moans of gratification from Michaelson's true believers, repelled the woman. Yet, she felt something warm happening below where Elaine had struck.

"Okay," Michaelson said. "Enough of this. Bring her."

Elaine grabbed the woman by the hair and neck and pushed her out of the room to follow Michaelson to the stairs.

"Us too, boss?" Hobbs asked.

"No," Michaelson growled. "*Us too, boss* can take my BMW to auto-detailing like they should have yesterday."

"Sure thing, boss," Hobbs said, motioning for Costa to follow him. Michaelson and the two women headed upstairs.

"I told you guys," Frank said to Lyedecker and Veretti,"You can't make me do anything bad anymore. I'll help you with some things, but not killing people."

"Well, maybe you can help us both by just shutting up," Lyedecker said standing over him.

Frank gave him a defiant smile.

"How long are we going to be holding this guy?" Veretti asked Lyedecker.

"You got some hot date or something?"

"I could have finished *A Tale of Two Cities*," Veretti said, eyeing the volume on the shelf above him, "if I had started reading it when we got here."

"*Two Cities*?" Lyedecker questioned. "You seem more like the *Batman and Robin* type."

"Actually, I read a lot of *Betty and Veronica* comics as a boy. I was a Betty man."

As the two bodyguards' intellectual discussion continued, Frank sat silent, knowing that he was about to be led to the guillotine like the *Two Cities* hero was.

"Speaking of Veronica," Lyedecker said, "Michaelson keeps talking about meeting this special Veronica babe. When's that ever going to happen?"

"She's not real," Veretti said. "None of that Arizona meteor pow-wow myth is real."

"How would you know?"

"That's just the hocus-pocus this group uses, along with ready-snatch, to get stupid people, like Frank here, to join."

"Bullshit," Lyedecker said. "We're all smarter, no? We're all stronger, no? And we're all richer, too."

"Yeah," Veretti agreed. "But have any of us ever seen ..."

The door opened and Michaelson walked in alone. Lyedecker and Jack straightened to attention.

Frank looked up from his chair but didn't stand as the final arbitrator approached him. As a soon to be condemned man he looked at

Michaelson's hand, wondering if it held a gun, needle, rope or a switch connected to 2,000 volts.

"So," Michaelson said, towering over Frank, "I hear you don't want to contribute to our group."

"It's not that. I'll be ...

"Haven't we treated you like family? Haven't I given you and everyone what I promised?

"Yes, it's true. It's just ..."

"All I've asked, all I've ever asked, is that everyone who gains from my support, carry out a few simple tasks for the greater good of all."

"I've done everything you've asked, but I can't anymore."

"Don't you want to stay with us? We've got great things happening here. And soon, very soon, we're being honored with a visit from Veronica herself."

Lyedecker and Veretti looked at each other and then back at Michaelson.

"You mean, she's real?" Veretti asked inadvertently.

"She's real," Michaelson assured him. "And Veronica has power," he said to Frank. "Real power on earth." He walked over to the window and looked out at the tree filled hills behind his large backyard area.

Frank swiveled his chair to follow him.

Lyedecker and Veretti kept their eyes on Frank in case he tried to run.

"When she does arrive," Michaelson continued, "she'll see that our group is the best. The best of all the other groups of our kind. And when she sees and knows that, she'll make me chief administrator over everyone. And then finally, after all these years ... for the first time ..."

Lyedecker and Veretti momentarily took their eyes off of Frank and looked at Michaelson waiting for his grand conclusion. But none came.

Michaelson came out of his rapture, took a deep breath, turned and looked directly into Frank's eyes. "If you cannot, for reasons of your own, continue with us, then that's okay. You can quit the group." He chuckled. "I guess there would be more than a couple of our female members who'll be sad to see you go."

"Yeah, boss," Veretti chuckled along with him, "There's this one girl who ..."

"So," Michaelson said, interrupting Veretti "You're free to go."

"What?" Frank said, moving to stand up. But Michaelson motioned him to remain seated. "You're serious? I can go?" But in the back of his mind, Jack knew that he was standing on a trap door, thirteen steps up over a prison yard, hands tied, parson reading.

"Yes, you can go," Michaelson said, "We have someone to take your place."

The long five-foot-fall to the end, before the rope snapped, Frank figured. "What?"

"Bring her in," Michaelson called out.

Frank swiveled his chair to face the door just in time to see the young woman come busting into the room, having been pushed by Elaine.

Frank jumped up in shock when he saw his sister. "Carolyn? Oh, Jesus. What the hell?"

Elaine walked in. "Yeah, Frank. What the hell?"

Caroline's tear stained face showed the remaining pain of Elaine's stomach punch and the psychic pain of having just seen that misty room. "Frank. What's going on?" she cried. "These people came and got me."

Frank jumped up and put his arms around her, then turned to Michaelson. "What the hell is this, Michaelson?"

"That's, Mister Michaelson, if you want to stay in my good graces."

"All right, Mister Michaelson. You've got me. I knew you would somehow. Just let us leave and I'll do what you want tomorrow."

"Bullshit," Veretti said, "You'll do what ..."

Michaelson's raised hand stopped Veretti. "I'm afraid, tomorrow isn't good enough, Frank. Your sister stays with us until you complete your mission."

"Let her go, please."

"It's simple, Frank," Michaelson said. "Drive the car and we let her go. If you don't ..."

"Please, not a mall full of people."

"Your sister can go and watch you accomplish your mission in person. Or, she'll be leashed up in our recruiting room until you decide to do the job. It's up to you."

"Frank," Carolyn said shaking, "They have a room full of women and ..."

"Yeah," Elaine jumped in. "Bet you never saw anything like that up close and ..."

"Let her go," Frank cried out.

"Come on, Frank," Michaelson said gently. "Get this done so the both of you can go home."

Frank plopped back down in the chair. "Oh, no. Jesus, how did this happen?"

"Okay, Frank," Veretti said. "In the words of the great Yogi Berra, 'It's *deja vu* all over again'."

"First let my sister leave. I don't want her to see this," Frank begged sitting in the car facing the Southgate shopping mall a quarter-mile ahead. Elaine held Carolyn by the hair on the sidewalk with a clear view of the mall.

"Nah," Veretti said. "She's gotta watch. Michaelson's orders. Now let's go through this one more time. Our man is standing by at the entrance with a pair of bolt cutters to cut the locks off the two center barrier poles and pull them out. So, there's nothing to stop you. All you have to do is crash inside the mall as far as you can go, hit the button and run. You've got a good eight seconds to get out of there, like I said."

"Eight seconds. Jesus," Frank said.

"Don't worry," Lyedecker said, standing behind Veretti. "Eight seconds is longer than you think. You'll have plenty of time."

"Don't do it," Carolyn called out to him. "I don't care wh ..."

A punch in the back from Elaine, stopped her words. "I can do this all day," Elaine said. She knew to keep her punches low and out of sight of any pain-in-the-ass, civic-minded pedestrians. "In fact, I'd love to do this all day with you."

From the side window of the car, Frank saw the jerking of Carolyn's head and knew she had been hit. "Leave her alone," he yelled to Elaine.

Lyedecker called his lock-cutting man on his phone. "Okay, get those poles out."

"Start her up, Frank," Veretti demanded. "Once those poles are removed, it won't be long till security comes to check it out, so we do this now."

Frank reluctantly turned the ignition key. "You guys are really bastards."

"It's now or your sister is screwed. Literally," Veretti threatened. "Over and over."

"The poles are out," Lyedecker said getting off his phone. "You've got a straight shot right now."

"Floor it, Frank," Veretti growled. "We want to see you go deep into that mall. And you damned well better hit the button before you run."

"Oh, Jesus," Frank yelled and hit the accelerator sending the car and him straight toward the mall doors.

"No, Frank. Stop," Carolyn yelled at the back of the accelerating car.

"Just watch," Elaine ordered. "This is gonna be fun."

"He'll jump, won't he?" Carolyn asked.

"Yeah, he'll jump. He's an energetic boy. He banged me a couple of times, so I should know."

As Frank sped into the parking lot, he hit his horn and held it. Shoppers with baskets, scattered. He dodged one lady and then hit the end of a cart full of groceries. A wine bottle flew at his windshield and shattered on it. But none of that mattered to the car's progress as Frank held both the horn and accelerator down hard.

He saw that the barrier poles were indeed gone. *Can I make it between the remaining poles?* Frank thought. The car sped through them with only inches to spare. He hit the doors. Shattered glass and busted metal flew past him. Oh, *Christ, this isn't happening,* Frank thought as he hit a young couple who barely had time to turn and know what was about to send them both flying dead through a shop window.

Some shoppers managed to scatter away from the speeding car but not the woman in the jewelry stand in the center of the mall. She had heard the car horn, the breaking door and the people screaming. But the surreal sight of a car in the mall barreling down on her froze her behind the jewelry case that, when hit by the car, became part of her as they were flattened together on the floor.

The juice stand that came next, was built solid and though tile, bricks and oranges went flying, the car came to a crashing stop.

Okay, push the button and run, Frank thought. *But what if I don't push it. What if I just run and tell Lyedecker that something must have gone wrong with the triggering mechanism?*

Frank hesitated his thumb over the button.

Then it occurred to him; *Maybe this button really doesn't matter. Maybe they've got this rigged so that they trigger it remotely. Blow me up with the car to keep me from talking.*

In the final white-flash, split-second, of his life, Frank understood that's exactly what they had done to him.

CHAPTER 10

1

"I've forgotten what a small, dull place this is," Veronica said.

Don slowed down their rental jeep as they approached Winslow. "Nice and quiet. And yeah, it's small all right."

"Too small for me," Veronica said.

"Yeah, for me too," Don agreed, as he did with everything she said. "The 'welcome to' and the 'you are now leaving' signs are on the same post."

"What?"

Don figured that the levity part of her brain was still not functioning, so he didn't bother explaining. "So, how was it living here?"

"I was raised at the reservation. I just wanted to see the town to help me remember."

"Oh, yeah. How's that going. Are you remembering more?"

"I remember why I left here when I was sixteen. That's for sure."

"So, why did you leave?"

"As soon as I saw the light, I knew I'd be off to big cities once I was old enough."

"Sounds like you got some inspiration from somebody or something? What was it?"

"The light, one night out in the desert."

"Sounds intriguing. What do you mean?"

"Stop the car."

"Sure." Don gently hit the brakes and came to a slow stop. He looked at her and saw she was eyeing something on the other side of the street.

She opened the door and got out. "Wait here."

"Okay. But are you all right?"

"I'll be back." She headed to the opposite side of the street.

Don rolled down his window. "What's up?"

Veronica didn't reply, but he could see that she was walking in the direction of some old farmer-type guy who was putting a sack of something in the back of his beat-up, pickup truck.

The man had a burnt-from-the-sun face under a straw cowboy hat. He opened the cab door, but before getting in, he felt the presence that was walking toward him. He turned to see the dark piercing eyes that he had last seen when she was around thirteen. Those eyes that had scared him then and were scaring him now. "It's you, isn't it?"

Veronica didn't speak until her face was a mere foot from his. "You have a good memory. You recognized me even though I've grown up."

"Your eyes."

"How have you been?"

"Ah, yes ... yes I am," he said, knowing he wasn't making sense.

"Am what?"

"I'm good. Fine."

She could see the sweat forming on his forehead and loved it. "Have you been following my orders?"

"Of course. Yes. I'm always on the lookout."

"Anyone asking about me?"

"Ah, well..."

"Anyone at all?"

"Well, there was this city guy."

"What did he want?"

"He just asked about you. That's all."

"And did you kill him?"

"I tried, but ..."

She inched her face closer. "But what?"

"He pulled a gun on me, so I couldn't do anything."

"Where is he?"

"I drove him to the Amtrak station in Flagstaff. That's the last I saw of him."

"Did you tell him anything about me?"

"No. Nothing. I swear."

She gently put her hand on his cheek. "Nothing?"

He took off his hat and pointed to one of two scars on the upper part of his forehead. "This says I didn't say anything." He pointed to the other one. "And this says I didn't. The guy smashed my head on a table, then hit me with a rock."

"What's his name?"

"I don't know. Some blond guy in his twenties."

She moved and gave him a gentle kiss on the cheek. "All right. You stay on guard now."

"Always. You can count on me."

She turned to go back across the street saying, "You can go back to your boring life now."

"Thank you."

"Who was that?" Don asked as Veronica got back into the jeep.

"An old boyfriend. I've got him in bondage."

2

"I'll be in China soon," Don said, tossing another pile of dirt next to the hole. "How far do you want me to go?"

"That's enough," Veronica replied, looking into the hole that she rightly figured would yield nothing. "I was just curious."

Don got out of the three-foot hole that he dug up with a broken shovel they found in Veronica's old fire-gutted barn. It had taken them an hour to drive out to the reservation from Winslow. Now in front of her also fire-gutted, old house, Don tossed down the shovel. "Curious about what?"

"My father told me he had some jewelry and gold buried here. But of course, he was lying. I just can't trust you people."

"You people? What did I do?"

"You were born on the wrong planet, like my father."

"Well, whatever that means."

"It just means I'm on my own."

"If you had mentioned what was supposed to be down here, I could have told you your father was probably just trying to show off."

"I knew it. But I wanted to be sure."

"Look, we don't have to worry about money. I'm doing good. I can take care of you."

"I can take care of myself."

"I'm sure you can, but you see, I think we ..."

"Are you aware this is reservation land?" came a female voice from behind them. "And it's off limits to everyone except those who live here?"

Veronica and Don turned to see a tall, beautiful Native American woman in her twenties giving them a stern look.

Veronica took a step forward, but when she saw the woman move her hand slowly for the sheathed knife on her hip, she stopped.

"I think it's a good idea for you two to move on," the woman said. "There's nothing her for you, so you can stop digging."

Veronica looked at the woman and then the shack that was behind her. Could it be Charlie and Koko's baby girl? "Tayanita?" Veronica asked pointing to the shack. "Are you Tayanita?

"Who are you?"

"You moved away, after that night," Veronica remembered.

"I lived in Texas for a while, but I came back a couple of years ago. So, who are you?"

"That's right," Veronica said. "You were just two or three when you left. I remember when your mother took you away."

The woman relaxed her hand, her eyes focusing inward for a moment. Then her eyes refocused on Veronica. "Chumana?"

"You remember me?"

"Just a little. But my mother talked a lot about your family and this place."

Veronica smiled, like a rattlesnake to a mouse. "Well, I was Chumana. But I'm Veronica Hawthorn now. No more Snake Woman."

"I'm Connie now," the woman said. "No more Beaver Maiden."

"And I thought Snake Woman was bad."

"Yeah," Connie said. "The boys thought my name was an invitation."

Don stood his ground waiting to be introduced.

"Speaking of boys," Veronica said, pointing to Connie's wedding band. "Looks like your married."

"Yeah. Johnny Lightcloud. He's in jail for the next four months."

"What for?"

"For being stupid."

"Any children."

"No, and I don't plan to," Connie said. "So, who's your friend?"

Veronica gave a 'doesn't matter' shrug of her shoulders.

"I'm Don Hoffman from Ferngrove, Washington. Veronica's staying with me for the time being."

Connie nodded.

Don looked over at Veronica who kept her eyes on Connie. Being forced to talk or just stand there, he volunteered, "You're always welcome to visit us and stay over, if you ever get up to Washington."

"You can take off now," Veronica said.

"What?" Connie asked. "What's your problem?"

"Not you," Veronica said to Connie. She turned to Don. "You. Take off."

Don looked at Veronica, then Connie, then back to Veronica. "What are you talking about?"

"You heard me," Veronica said coolly. "Just turn and start walking."

"What do you mean?"

Veronica turned her attention back to Connie. "I'd like to talk to you about the old days."

"Sure," Connie said. "I'd like that."

"I thought we were together," Don said.

"I can't help what you think."

Don reached out gently to take her arm. "Look, I've been very help ...."

With viper-like speed, she grabbed him by the throat. "Walk or dig a deeper hole."

Connie had seen a lot of outrageous things done by men on the reservation, but this reversal of roles was something she wanted to see play out, whether this guy ended up in the hole or not.

"Okay, okay," he managed to get the words out. "Let go."

Veronica released her iron grip on him.

Don took three steps back from her holding his throat. "What's gotten into you all of a sudden?"

"You'd be surprised what's gotten into me, and not so far from here," Veronica said, turning her back to him.

"I don't know what you're talking about," Don said still catching his breath.

"You're not supposed to."

Connie was enjoying this and wishing she had some of whatever Veronica had going for her.

"What's the idea of having me bring you all the way out here just to drop me cold?"

"You were useful. Now I have a new friend."

Connie liked the sound of that, even though she was now equating Veronica's breaking up with a boyfriend, like a female praying mantis eats the head off of the male while he's impregnating her, instinctively knowing that, headless, he'll thrust harder and deliver more semen. Cold bitches both. Yet, weirdly fascinating. And in Veronica's case, to Connie, fascinating and immediately attractive.

"A new friend?" Don asked. "I don't get it."

Connie decided to join in on the female domination fun with, "And it looks like you won't getting it anymore. Not from her anyway."

"I like that," Veronica said to Connie, smiling at her. Then she turned to Don. "Okay. That's it. Take off."

Don, now speechless for being a fool and letting himself be used by a stranger, hung his head and started walking toward the jeep.

"Leave the jeep," Veronica demanded.

"Are you crazy? How am I going to get back?"

"Your problem. Not mine."

Don's mind tried to search out and select just the right farewell insult to tell this bitch. But not wanting to feel her death-grip again, he turned to Connie and asked, "Which direction is Winslow?"

Amused, Connie pointed to the road he and Veronica had driven in on.

"Yeah, right." Don turned and slowly began walking.

Once he got out of earshot, Connie looked at Veronica with admiration and asked, "Who was that?"

"An ex-boyfriend. I had him in bondage."

"Yeah. That's where they all belong."

Veronica motioned to the jeep. "Want to take a ride?"

"Where to?"

"Not far from here. A place that will change your life."

"Oh?" Connie said, licking her lips. "I could use a place like that?"

"Good. Let's go."

"I guess you're talking about a casino. And I could use a drink after seeing what you did to that poor guy."

"Do you feel sorry for him?" Veronica asked.

"Not at all. I admire the style, the way you dropped him. Wish I could push men around like that."

Veronica gave a predatory smile. "The things I do, you too can do. And even greater things."

"Sounds intriguing," Connie said.

"It's the only verse I liked from my mother's bible readings."

"I thought that sounded familiar. Well lead me to the casino."

"This isn't gambling," Veronica said. "This is a sure thing."

Knowing that Don left the keys in the ignition, Veronica got in behind the wheel and started it up. Connie happily jumped in on the other side and they were off.

Seeing Don ahead of them walking down the dusty, single lane road, Veronica told Connie. "Grab that brown bag on the back seat and toss it out the window at him.

As they approached Don, Veronica blasted her horn at him without slowing down. Connie rolled down her window and tossed the small bag at him while giving a happy smile and sardonically funny wave good-bye.

Don was too heartsick and depressed about losing that incredible piece of erotica to be angry. He picked up his bag that did not hold anything much of value and continued on down the road.

He pulled out his phone, but there was no signal. He knew he wasn't in any danger unless her ran into another war party like the one he had just survived.

He had his wallet full of cash in his pocket, credit cards and I.D. He could probably hitch back to Winslow from the main road. From there, he could certainly arrange transport to Flagstaff, report the jeep stolen and fly back to Washington where a cold, empty bed awaited him.

My ex-wife made me go up in the Space Needle and then divorced me, he thought. *This one made me take her to Arizona and then left me to the wolves. Have they been worth it?* The image of Veronica approaching his bed nude, the second night she was there, unraveled that riddle, as far as she was concerned.

As for his ex-wife? Well, she wasn't worth that acrophobia producing elevator ride to the top of the Needle.

"So, where are we headed?" Connie asked Veronica in the now speeding jeep.

"You'll like it," Veronica assured her. She reached down into her bag and pulled out her Navajo doll.

"What's with the doll?"

"It's my surrogate father." Veronica held the doll in her left hand away from Connie's complete view.

"Surrogate father? Well, if you say so. I hope he treats you better than your real father."

"He was okay. He left me a treasure."

"Is that what you were digging up back there?"

"I made my boy-toy do the digging."

"Yeah, right. Did you find anything?"

"Gold and jewelry. Gold and jewelry and stuff," she assured Connie while she reached into the doll under its clothes, found the crystal and put her palm over it. "At least that's what I found there in my imagination."

Connie could see the concentration coming onto Veronica's face. "Anything wrong?"

"I'm just thinking about arranging a meeting."

"Are we going to meet someone today?"

"Tonight."

"Who?"

"Someone who'll show you the light and make you rich, strong and free."

"I'm game," Connie said. "As long as I don't have to give him my soul."

3

"So, what are we doing here?" Connie's words came out in a cold breath that lingered above the meteor crater for a second then disappeared.

"I thought this would be a quiet place to talk," Veronica answered as she looked at the moon just rising on the other side of the huge, round chasm.

"Sure, it's quiet. But this night air is really cold."

Veronica used that as an opportunity to sit down next to Connie already seated on a large rock. "Just to keep warm," she assured her.

Connie nodded while her eyes scanned the crater rim looking for an animal that might consider them dinner.

Veronica slowly slipped her arm around Connie's waist. Feeling that, Connie turned and looked Veronica in the eyes that were now only a few inches away.

"Just to stay warm," Veronica explained.

"So, what are we doing out here?"

"We're going to be partners."

"I hope it's not partners in crime. I don't want to join my husband in jail," Connie said, turning her head back to animal watching.

"Oh, no. Not crime." Veronica moved her lips closer to Connie's ear and whispered. "Partners in owning the world."

"If it means money, I'm all for it."

"It means money and a lot more."

"I'll take the *more*, as long as it starts with *money*." Connie ventured another turn of her head to look into Veronica's eyes. "But what does that have to do with being out here in this cold? You said we're going to meet someone."

"We will. Just wait and everything will be clear."

This time Connie could not turn her head away. *Those eyes,* she thought.

Veronica moved her arm from Connie's waist up to her shoulder and gently squeezed it.

"What's that sound?"

"You can hear that?" Veronica asked.

"It's a kind of humming."

"Yes, I hear it, too."

Connie looked up into the star filled sky to where it seemed the sound was coming from. Something large and dark was blocking some of the stars. The humming increased its intensity. More stars were being blocked. Whatever was descending was starting to show its shape.

"What is that?" Connie asked. "Something's ..."

"Just look at it and relax."

"What's that light?

"Just keep looking."

"It's beautiful."

The only thing that Connie could remember from that night was Veronica holding her like a mother holds a child for a vaccination.

4

The tom-toms and chanting brought Connie half-out of her trance and staring into the face of a feather-headed chief that had to be at least ninety. In full Indian regalia, he had his hands on each side of Connie's face saying something in a native tongue that she couldn't discern.

She wanted to back away from this painted father-of-time, but her feet seemed frozen in the red rock that flickered from the light of several flaming torches.

Connie saw Veronica standing next to her in a white rabbit-fur robe with a proud and satisfied expression. Turning her head to the right a little, she saw two Indian maidens also in white fur.

Connie couldn't see who were beating on the tom-toms and chanting as they were behind her, but it sounded like at least three men.

After a few more words, the old man let go of her face. A young half-naked Indian man handed the old man a chipped pottery bowl which he put up to Connie's mouth. He said something to her, and then pressed the bowls to her lips. She knew it had to mean *drink*, so she drank what tasted like cactus mixture.

Seemingly satisfied, the man handed the bowl back to the young man and then gestured to the natural hot spring that was on the rocks just below the group.

"Take off your robe," Veronica said solemnly.

Connie looked down to see she was also wearing white fur. She moved it off her shoulders and let it drop to the rock. She noticed that the chief didn't react to her nudity, too old or too spiritual maybe. But it seemed to her that the men were beating their tom-toms a little faster.

Veronica raised her arm pointing downward to the bubbling thermal spring in the rocks a few steps down. "Connie."

Connie carefully made her way down and entered the steaming spring.

Veronica turned to the other two young women extending her hand toward them. "Odina."

Veronica's childhood friend dropped her robe and followed Connie.

"Little Bird," Veronica said.

Little Bird, who never minded the jokes about her name and even encouraged them, used to be shy about having to use the outside public shower in front of other reservation children. But now she was older and proud of what nature had done for her. She ever so slowly dropped her robe, more for teasing the young men chanting, then for getting ready to enter the spring.

Veronica, who long ago found out that she was more powerful undraped than draped, was happy to shed her skins and follow her new and old disciples into the bubbling water.

In the thermal spring, Veronica moved behind Connie who was still half in a trance. She put an arm around Connie's chest and, in a low voice, just audible above the sound of the warm bubbles, said, "Don't worry. The effects of your awakening will end soon, and you will be born into a wonderful world where you can have anything you want, as long as you serve our master."

Veronica motioned to Odina and Little Bird. They moved in the water to the front of Connie and wrapped their arms around her as well.

Veronica looked up in the sky, taking a moment to breathe in the sulfur steam that was surrounding all four of them. Then she tightened her hug on Connie, pressing herself against Connie's back, moving her lips next to Connie's ear and whispering. "We are sisters. Always together. All challengers defeated. All fears tranquilized. All boredoms entertained. All desires gratified."

CHAPTER 11

1

"I have to get back to my place to pick up the rest of my pistols and more ammo," Chang said mostly to Angela, though Cathy and Miles were also there in George's cabin.

"You didn't think to take them all with you when you left," Miles asked.

Chang turned to Miles. "When we left, I thought we'd be laying low for a while in Vancouver and then return once the heat was off. I didn't figure we'd be on the run possibly forever."

George walked into the cabin. "The manager just told me a hell of a thing."

"What," Cathy asked expecting the bad news that was already printed on George's face.

"It was on the radio ..."

"What now?" Miles asked.

"It seems," George said, "someone drove a car full of explosives into the Southgate Mall."

Cathy plopped down on a chair. "Oh, no."

Chang and Angela turned to look at each other. She was about to speak, but the slight shake of his head stopped her.

"How many were ...?" Miles stopped himself.

"I don't want to say," George said.

Angela moved toward her husband. "And I don't want to know."

Cathy started searching it on her phone.

"One thing's for sure," George said, "it has to be Michaelson's group that did it."

"We can guess that, George," Miles said. "But we don't know that for sure."

"Come on, Miles," George said. "Any act of destruction in Washington or Oregon has to be Michaelson's doing. That mall is most likely publicly owned with stocks dropping as we speak."

"Yeah, it is publicly owned," Miles conceded. "The Tyler Corporation."

"Michaelson's most likely got short bids on that stock and is counting his profits right now," George said.

"We'd better stop our plan, George," Cathy said.

"Stop nothing," Chang jumped in. "We're going to hit them hard."

"Right," George agreed.

Miles stepped forward. "Are you sure about this? Do you really think we can walk right into this guy's house and walk out with his computer and blessings?"

"We don't need any of his blessings," Chang said. "So let's get back to it."

"We're still short-handed," George said to Chang. "We've got Angela and Miles here going into the house, Cathy driving and on surveillance. That just leaves you and me outside the house to go in if trouble happens."

"It better not happen," Miles said.

"Yeah, you're right," Chang said. "Just the two of us to cover a two-story house isn't enough." Chang walked over to the rough layout of the house pinned to the wall. "I'm not sending Angela in there with just a two-man back up. We'll need two or three more. Two men for each floor and one in reserve."

"Well, there's only two of us for that," George said.

"We need to hire a couple more guys," Chang said.

"You mean like mercenaries?" asked George.

Chang turned to look at George. "Or any man that needs the money. You can pay them, right?"

"How much will it take, do you think?" George asked.

"Say about, twenty-five thousand a piece."

"I've got that right here," George said. "In my pocket and in my bag."

Chang looked at his watch, then grabbed his pistol. "How far is Ella Baily park from here?"

2

"How many times a day do you take breaks, Mr. Gomez?" asked the plump, middle-aged woman in a park uniform approaching him.

"This is only the second time I've sat down all day, Miss Blair," Gomez lied. He was used to lying and making people believe him. Sometimes they didn't believe him. One of those times landed him in prison for fifteen years.

Gomez was fifty-three, covered in prison *tats* and destined to live the rest of his job-life as a state park janitor. Though better than being a state convict, he missed the respect that he got from his inmates.

"Well, when you feel up to starting again," Blair said, "you'll have to sweep around there, all around there and over there. And before that, empty the trash box before it overflows."

"You secretly like me, don't you Miss Blair?" Gomez said with a straight face.

"That's irrelevant to whether the trash box gets emptied," she said, controlling a smile.

"Irrelevant?" Gomez mimicked. "You sound like the prosecutor who sent me up-river."

"Never mind who I sound like."

"Hey, Miss Blair. Do you know why they say sent him *up-river*?"

"Isn't that amazing, Mr. Gomez. I woke up this morning wondering why they say '*up-river*'."

"I learned it in the joint. They said '*up-river*' when they sent guys to Sing-Sing prison on the Hudson."

"Well, now that you've graduated from '*the joint*' university, and I've been enlightened," Blair said walking away, "let's see if you can earn your degree in sanitation."

Gomez laughed and called out to her, "Say, do you think a guy like me and a girl like you ...?" He purposely stopped.

"It would never work," she said without looking back.

That's nice, Gomez thought. *I can trade jokes without having to edit myself for fear of getting knifed in the showers.*

He stood up, grabbed his broom, and walked over to the almost overflowing trash box in the middle of the park.

"I guess it beats cleaning up cell blocks," a voice from the distance called to Gomez.

He turned to see, a well-built Asian guy and some blond guy carrying cups of coffee. "What the ..." He squinted his eyes to focus. "Chang? Is that you?"

"How's it going number 47283624," Chang said approaching.

"Oh, man, Chang. How could you remember my number?"

"You doing okay?"

"Cleaning up here or the big house. What's the *diff*?"

Chang handed him a cup of coffee. "Black, the way you like it."

Gomez let his broom fall to the grass and took it. "Black was the only way we could get it inside. Remember?"

"I remember."

Gomez lifted the plastic lid on the cup, as was his prison habit. One learns to look before one ingests anything in prison. Seeing it was indeed coffee, he took a sip. He eyed George but waited for an introduction. "And what have you been doing since you got sprung?"

"I opened a school," Chang said, "teaching what you taught me."

"Yeah? Well, that's good. Wish I could be your assistant. But my circle-back-kick is a little slow these days."

"Mine's almost non-existent," Chang said.

"And my left-hand punching is not so great since the boys did a number on me. Remember that time you pulled them off me?"

"Sure do. Too many of 'em that day."

"Yeah, my arm is still messed up and I get a little fuzzy sometimes. But I'm still good. Kicked out some guys throwing snowballs at people last year. I love throwing guys out of my park."

Chang pointed to George. "This is one of my students, George. He wants to pay you twenty-five thousand dollars for a one-day job."

Gomez stopped in the middle of large sip of coffee. "Well now. That would be a lot of donuts for this coffee, which you didn't bring."

"Sorry about that," Chang said. "Next time an assortment."

"Twenty-five thousand dollars." Gomez said. "What's the catch?"

"The catch is that us three will stand by for a possible raid on a nest of terrorists," George said.

"That's not the catch," Gomez smiled, That's the fun."

"You mentioned your arm," George said, "And that you're 'a little fuzzy'?"

"My gun holding arm is fine. So is my trigger finger. And I'm only a little fuzzy when I'm bored."

"We need one more man," Chang said. "What about Flypaper?"

"Nah. Flypaper died in the joint."

"Oh. Sorry to hear," Chang said. "Anyone else you can think of without a family, who needs twenty-five grand?"

"No. All still inside. Or dead."

Chang looked at George. "We'll just have to make do with us three."

"I'll have that twenty-five grand up front. I want to give it to my daughter."

"Daughter?" Chang questioned. "Why you never ... Chang stopped to think."Say, maybe this isn't such a good idea for you."

Gomez ignored Chang's suggestion and asked George, "Can you get me the cash right away?"

George eyed him with concern, but then answered. "Yes."

"All right. It's your call," Chang conceded. "Let's go to my school and pick up some more weapons."

"Hey, you didn't say we'd have to fight with nunchucks," Gomez said.

"Weapons that need ammo," Chang assured him.

"Right." Gomez tossed his remaining coffee on the grass, threw the cup in the trash box. "Just kidding, I can see the pistol bulges under your shirts."

"Good," Chang said. "You've still got your edge."

"I still got my eyes," Gomez said.

"Our car's this way," George said.

"Okay," Gomez said happily. "Maybe I could get a shave and haircut. And a bullet proof vest."

"We got vests," George said.

"Mr. Gomez," came Miss Blair's voice from behind them. "Where are you going?"

The three men stopped and turned. Gomez trotted over to where he dropped his broom, picked it up and handed it to Blair. "Be sure to sweep all around there," he pointed. "And all around there. And all around there."

Blair reluctantly took the broom handle. "But first I should empty the trash?" she asked wryly.

"Yes," Gomez said. "Before it overflows." He trotted back to walk off with George and Chang.

"Good luck, Mr. Gomez. Stay safe," she said with real concern. She saw Gomez turn and start trotting back in her direction. She froze as he approached, tightening her body for whatever was to come.

Gomez planted a soft kiss on her check that was longer than just a peck, then trotted back to George and Chang.

Blair stood there, broom in hand, watching Gomez walk off while she controlled a smile that wanted to come out.

"My pistols are already bagged," Chang told George and Gomez as they headed down the alley steps that lead to his karate school. "I'll be back out in less than two minutes. I just have to grab a few extra things, as well."

On the way down the cement stairs the three men kept an eye out for anyone that might be part of Michaelson's group. Knowing it was risky, but needing more weapons, Chang figured it was worth a chance to grab what they needed with only a few moments of exposure.

Looking around the stairs, there was a couple of children sitting on the the steps looking at comic books. A young man was talking to what looked to be his girlfriend. There were also a middle-aged couple, who looked to be locals, walking up the stairs. But no one suspicious.

Chang pulled out his keys. As they approached the entrance to his school. He unlocked and opened the door. George and Gomez turned to watch the alley.

"Okay, stand by," Chang said entering and closing the door.

"How about you watch upstairs and I watch down?" George said to Gomez.

"Right," Gomez, said leaning against the wall. He took a second look at the guy and his girlfriend. Locals for sure, but your never know who might be working for the other side, as he learned in prison. "So, you said this guy Michaelson saw you two head off in a boat?"

"Yeah," George said, keeping his eyes peeled in the opposite direction. "But he's no fool. He knows there's a chance that we got off and returned to the city. Which we have."

"Well, I'll feel better when we get out of Chinatown and I get my hands on some weapons."

"I've got mine ready," George assured him.

The seconds ticked slowly away as they waited for Chang. Finally, to fill the silence, George asked "So, you met Mr. Chang in prison, huh? We're you cellmates?"

"What most people really want to know is what I was in for."

"I'm just breaking the ice."

"I'm your soldier. Not your date."

George chuckled. "Right you are."

"Well, it was manslaughter and a few other things, if that's all right with ..." Gomez saw two men coming down the stairs toward them. One tall, one stocky wearing jackets and ties. "Who are these two guys?"

"George turned and looked to see two men."I don't know. They're not locals, I don't think."

Gomez said quietly. "And they don't look like tourists."

George moved his hand slowly toward his pistol under his shirt.

"Freeze," came the sudden yell from the stocky man who had been concealing a pistol behind him that was now pointed at Gomez.

The tall man quickly pulled his pistol from under his jacket and aimed it at George.

"Not one muscle," the stocky man said approaching. The playing children didn't see anything happening, but the guy with his girlfriend saw, took her hand and guided her up the stairs. The tall man saw them, but knew they were of no consequence.

"All right, boys," the stocky man said, "The pistols. Dump 'em."

George slowly moved his hands up. "I'm clean, man."

"I see the bulge," the tall man said to George. "Left hand. Dump it."

George complied. His pistol hit the ground.

The tall man pointed his gun at Gomez. "Now you. Drop the pistol slowly."

"I don't have one," Gomez said.

"You don't have one?" the tall man repeated. "Well, you'd better find one."

"I'm clean man." Gomez slowly lowered his hands.

"Watch it," the stocky man warned.

Gomez slowly lifted his park uniform shirt showing bar skin. He slowly turned around to prove he didn't have any weapons.

"Okay, now where's that other guy?" the stocky man asked, gritting his teeth.

"Is this a stick up?" George asked. "Or are you with Michaelson?"

"Never mind that. Just move away ..."

The door behind George and Gomez burst open surprising the two men. With his enhanced speed, strength and Chang's training, George was on the stocky man like lightning, grabbing his pistol away from him and shooting the startled taller man in the chest before he could fire.

George turned to the stocky man and hit him on the head with the butt of the gun. The man fell to the ground stunned, but conscious. George scooped up his pistol from the ground and tossed it to Gomez. The playing children screamed and ran up the stairs away from danger.

"What the hell, Chang?" Gomez squawked. "You didn't hear them?"

"Me?" Chang growled. "You let yourself get caught like this?"

"Hey, don't get on ..." Before Gomez could finish, the stocky man got up and painfully started climbing the stairs holding his head. Coming down the stairs came an elderly Asian man with a bag of groceries in his arms. The man froze when he saw the injured man staggering up the stairs toward him.

Chang laid down his weapons bag, pulled out his pistol and aimed it at the wounded man's back as he approached the elderly man.

"Let him go, Chang," George said.

Chang whispered to himself, "I am a bullet," and pulled the trigger.

Chang's spirit-filled projectile hit the man in the back of the neck, dropping him at the elderly man's feet. The elderly man must have seen it all in his lifetime and must have valued his groceries as well, because he restarted his decent down the stairs to his home.

Chang quickly locked the door to his school and picked up his bag. "We can get to the car around back." He began to head down the stairs. Not feeling Gomez and George behind him, he turned and saw them standing frozen with bewildered expressions.

"What is it?" Chang asked them, still with grim determination on his face.

"Jesus, Chang," Gomez muttered.

"He was going back to Michaelson's to report us," Chang said.

George looked back upstairs at the dead body, then back to the man's body that he killed. "I had to kill this one," he said to Chang. "Sure, that guy would have reported us, but still."

"Screw 'em," Chang yelled. "They're all terrorists, aren't they?"

George looked back up the stairs where some of the local people were gathering to satisfy their curiosity. Gomez continued to stare at Chang.

"What are you looking at? My wife and I were at the Southgate Mall just two weeks ago," Chang said. He repeated shouting, "Just two weeks ago."

"Let's get out of here," Gomez said.

The three of them descended the stairs as two children passed them, running up to check out just another two bodies in Chinatown.

CHAPTER 12

1

Steve Sorenson was a 22-year-old college graduate backpacking and hitching his way through California. He had started off with three of his dorm-mates in San Diego. Two made it as far as San Francisco, with the third one dropping out when they reached Napa. It seems that his buddies were more interested in getting back to their hometown girlfriends than to enjoy what the road had to offer.

Steve did have a girl waiting for him back in San Diego, but he wanted to complete his plans of ending up at Mt. Shasta for swimming and boating. After that, he would fly back home.

His last ride had left him off at Red Bluff on Highway 5, which put him about 90 miles from his destination. He had walked about 10 miles from there and was now in the mood for a ride, hopefully with some tourists, all the way to Shasta.

About twenty cars ignored his thumb and then came the hitchhiker's dream, a large, brand-new recreation vehicle. That meant, depending on the generosity of the owner, possible water, food, beer, restroom and maybe even a shower. *And look*, he thought. *It's slowing down. It's stopping.*

The Winnebago Horizon pulled off the road and came to a smooth stop next to him. The door opened with the two steps moving out like they were inviting him. Looking in, Steve could see that the driver was a tan-skinned woman with long black hair and beautiful.

"What a ride?" Odina asked.

"I didn't have my thumb out to test the wind," Steve joked to no reaction.

"Come aboard then."

Steve stepped up into the RV almost getting hit in the backside as Odina quickly closed the door behind him and stepped on the gas. "Where you headed?" he asked her.

"Does it matter?"

"I guess not, as long as it's north."

"Go on back and grab a beer."

"Super," he said turning to the back, "This is quite a rig you ..." The sight of Veronica, Connie and Little Bird sitting on the sofas in shorts and tank tops disconcerted him. More disconcerting to him though was Veronica not even looking up. She just continued painting her fingernails red.

She was sitting next to a snakeskin bag that had the head of a creepy looking doll sticking out of it. An old Indian man doll that seemed to be staring right at him.

Next to the bag sat Connie who had been thumbing through an old copy of People Magazine, but now looked up at him with the same intensity of that damned doll.

And Little Bird was just lying back on a large pillow with her brown legs on the sofa, checking him out like a coyote checks out a rabbit.

"Hello," he said. "Mind if I put my backpack down?"

Veronica finally looked up from her nails, nodded and pointed her nail brush at the floor. Steve took off his pack and laid it down. "I've Steve from San Diego."

All three women gave him a '*so what*' look.

"Yeah, so anyway," he continued. "I'm heading to Mt. Shasta. I'll rent a bike and also do some swimming there."

"That sounds nice," Little Bird said.

Finally, some response, he thought. "So, where are you all heading?"

"Seattle," Little Bird said.

Veronica gave her a sharp look.

A little stunned, Little Bird mouthed 'sorry' to her patron and then corrected herself to Steve. "I mean we're passing through there." But we can drop you off near Mt. Shasta."

"Yeah? Great. So, your driver happened to mention there's a beer back here for me."

"In the frig," Veronica pointed again with her brush.

"Thanks." Steve reached down and opened the small refrigerator. "Budweiser in bottles. Nice. Cold, too."

"The opener's right there," Little Bird said.

"Thanks," Steve said, grabbing a bottle and popping it open. "Well," he said holding the bottle out. "Here's to the open road." He took a big sip.

Little Bird was the only one to smile and acknowledge his toast.

"So, like I was going to say, this is a great RV. The best way to travel." He took another sip. "Better than going through the damned security checks for airplanes."

"That's exactly why we rented this thing," Veronica ventured. "But it gets boring all the way from Arizona."

"Yeah," Connie purred. "All those monotonous white lines on the road."

"Yeah," Steve smiled at her. "I guess I know what you mean. But those lines go by a lot slower when you're walking."

"So," Veronica said, putting a cap on her nail polish bottle and setting it down. "Are you more entertaining than those boring white lines?"

Steve figured she might be hinting at what he hoped she was. After all, this kind of stuff happened to him in the girls' dorm a couple of times. But he didn't want to jump the gun and get it wrong, so he said, "I'm pretty good with coin magic."

"That sound good," Veronica said. "Why don't you go back there, take a shower and come back and show my three friends here some magic?" She learned over and called out. "How about it, Odina? Steve's going to show us some magic. If you're interested, I can take over at the wheel for a while."

"Sounds good," Odina called back. "I could use a shot."

"Okay, Steve," Veronica said. "Take a shower and show them some magic."

"What about you?" he asked Veronica. "You're not interested in magic?"

"I am. But you couldn't handle my magic."

Steve smiled and headed back to the shower saying, "Well, whatever that means."

"Make if fast, will ya," Connie called to him. "Let's see what you can make disappear."

"I'll try," he called back.

"Yeah, well, try hard," one of them said. But he didn't know which one.

2

Two hours later, a middle-aged man was changing his tire on the side of the road. He heard a vehicle coming to a stop about twenty yards behind him. He turned to see an RV stopping, the door opening and a young man in his underwear come flying out, hitting the dirt, and groaning from the pain of it.

He saw the young man struggling to get to his feet and yelling at the open door, "What the hell are you whores do ..." He was cut off by a backpack being thrown at him, followed by a bundle of loose clothes hitting him in the face. "You damned bitches," the dusty, scraped up young man yelled, "I did what you wanted. I gave you all a ..."

"Fuck off," a woman's voice could be heard using a comical tone, followed by a laugh. The door slammed shut and the RV drove off.

3

"That's it," Cathy said, talking off her headphones. "Hey, guys," she called out the window of the cabin. "Come on in."

"What's happening?" George said as he entered followed by Chang, Angela and Miles. George moved over to where she was sitting behind one of the computers.

"They're going to have some kind of get-together on Thursday afternoon."

"That's two days from now," George said. "Are you sure?"

"Hey, not so close," Cathy said, annoyed that he was leaning over her. She was still angry at the situation George had literally screwed her into. "Someone at Michaelson's has been ordering food, alcohol and flowers. And then finally I heard a couple of invitations."

"What else could it be?" Angela said.

"Oh, brother," Miles said in a worried tone. "Here's where we start cookin'."

"Did you hear a time for the deliveries?" George asked.

"All in the morning," Cathy said.

"I guess that is it," George said. "The party I attended was in the afternoon. So, chances are it'll be held in the afternoon."

"Two days from now, huh?" Miles said.

Chang looked at Angela, then said to George, "If that's the case, then Angela and I have something we have to do on our own."

"What?" Angela asked.

"How long will you be gone?" George asked.

"Don't worry. We won't jeopardize any of our plans."

"Gee, Mr. Chang," Miles said. "Do you think you should leave now? I mean, it's getting pretty close."

"We'll be back tonight."

"Do what you have to, Mr. Chang," George said.

Chang took Angela by the hand, "Come on. The sooner we start, the sooner we'll be back."

Angela shook her head in wonderment. "Look, I know when I married you, that you liked to play 'the man of mystery', but sometimes you take it a little too far."

"Have you got a nice dress in that suitcase you've been dragging around?"

"Nice enough," she said. "Are you talking me to a champagne dinner or something?"

"Not exactly," Chang said, leading her out of George's cabin to theirs. "But a champagne dinner dress would do just fine."

"Oh, great," Miles said, once they were out of ear-range. "They get to go dating and I'm up here with the forest animals for company."

"Don't worry, Miles," Cathy said. "Maybe you'll find a nice date when you crash Michaelson's party."

"Angela's my date for that," Miles said.

"We'll maybe you'll get lucky with her," George joked.

"Right," Miles said. "And get *karate-cised* to death by that Neanderthal husband of hers?

4

A few minutes later, Angela looked beautiful in a light blue dressed. Chang didn't have a sports jacket, but at least he was out of his black leather jacket and wearing a grey shirt that Miles had picked up for him on one of his provision runs.

The couple were getting into the SUV as George and Cathy walked out of the cabin to see them off. "Take care," George said.

"You both look so nice," Cathy said.

Angela smiled at her.

They drove away. Cathy turned to head go to her cabin, but George gently took her arm. She didn't object to his nearness this time, but said, "You know, Miles is in there. You should be ..."

"Let's take a little walk and talk about things."

"I don't know, George." But she started walking as he lead her toward the forest that surrounded the cabins.

"You know," he said. "now that we are connected this way ..."

"I don't like this so-called connection. I didn't ask for it."

"I'm not talking about that. I'm sorry about what happened concerning that. It's just that you and I should be together."

"Why? Just because you say so? And that girl you met in San Francisco. You're still connected to her, aren't you?"

"I don't know about that."

"You were talking to her in bed with me. Going crazy. Obsessed."

"I'll never see her again."

"You see her in your mind. I can't compete with that. I wouldn't even be interested in competing with that. I don't think any woman would want to." She stopped walking, causing George to stop.

"Before we go back," he said. "I want to show you something."

"What?"

"Us." George slowly lifted both of his hands towards Cathy's heard in the manner that Veronica had done to him."

"What are you trying to ..."

"Hold still. Close your eyes."

"What are you doing?"

"Come on. Trust me."

She decided to oblige him and closed her eyes.

"Now make your mind a blank," George said as he concentrated inward.

"I don't ..." The power that went into her from George hands gave her a vison of a florescent pale-green wall in front of her. The wall dissolved to reveal something behind it. In her mind, she saw herself being introduced to George by her boss Raskin on her first day of work at the technology company.

"This is George Barrett. Team leader for your group."

"Nice to meet you," Cathy said.

George smiled. "Welcome to the salt mines."

"Hey come on," Raskin said.

She smiled slightly seeing that vison. With George's hands on her head, George continued sending memories into her brain.

She saw their first date, ice cream cones on Pier 57, then a ride on the giant Ferris wheel. Standing in the forest she could remember and feel the fear and excitement of it. The fear of falling from 175 feet from the top of the wheel. And the excitement of falling in love with George.

Then came the image of her and George at the top of the hill overlooking the city with the Space Needle in the center of it. "I used to come here often as a boy and just sit and watch the city lights," George said to her.

The next image Cathy saw was their first kiss in the elevator at her apartment building.

In the forest George watched Cathy smile during her hypnotic adventure. Now it was the two of them walking hand in hand at the Des Moines beach with the beautiful view of Puget Sound. The image of Cathy in bed under him gasping and ...

"Sorry," George said, talking his hands off her and letting the trance break. "I went a little too far."

Cathy took a moment to come back to reality and then said, "You always go too far, George. Much too far."

"Yeah, I guess maybe so."

"I remember everything, George. You didn't have to show me. I remember the feelings, too. But we're in trouble now. And I'm not just talking about Michaelson. And I'm afraid we ..."

She turned and headed back to her separate cabin.

CHAPTER 13

1

"Well, the convict finally shows up after all these years." Chang's brother Dillion said as he and Angela approach his parents' house.

On the forty-minute drive, Chang told Angela his plan to finally see them and introduce her to them. "You'd better call them before we arrive," she had suggested. But he figured he'd either be told not to come or they would want to make it sometime in the future. And for Chang and Angela, their future was uncertain.

He was lucky to have both of his parents alive in their mid-eighties. He hadn't seen them since he went to prison nor the two years that he'd been out. His mother had visited him twice when he was incarcerated, but her constant tears on those visits where too much for him, so he told her to stay way.

There were some sporadic letters from her with photos, but they gradually stopped.

As for his father? Total renouncement.

Now standing above him and Angela on his parents' front porch, was his 45-year-old brother Dillion.

Dillon had played it smart when they lived in Chinatown. Nothing too heavy that could get him years of incarceration. Just some small, two-bit scams, hustles and odd jobs that earned him beer and date money. Especially since his dates consisted of buying beers for his night's companionship.

"Ex-convict," Chang corrected Dillon. "And it's good to see you, too."

Dillon motioned his head at Angela. "Who's this?"

"This is my wife, Angela. Angela, this is my brother, Dillon. My best friend when we were kids."

Dillon softened a little. "Hello."

"It's nice to finally meet you," Angela said.

"I bet my brother told you a lot about me."

"Not exactly," Angela half-smiled.

"I told her nothing about nobody," Chang said.

"Does mom and dad know about her?"

"No," Chang said, looking-over the middle-class residence. "Well, the folks finally moved out of Chinatown. And mom finally got a yard."

"Backyard, too," Dillon volunteered.

"So, do we just stand here?" Chang asked. "Or do we come in?"

"No one's stopping you," Dillon said. "But they didn't mention you coming here, so I take it they don't know."

Chang guided Angela forward. "No. Best to jump into ice water quickly."

"Best for who?" Dillion asked.

"Better for all concerned," Chang said, approaching the screen door with the front door already opened. "Hey, mom. It's me," Chang called into the house. "Are you home, dad?"

"Who is it?" came a man's gruff voice.

"It's Kenneth," Chang called inside.

"Kenny?" came a woman's voice. Chang's mother came up to the door. She looked him and Angela over for a moment and then said, "Come in."

Chang pulled open the screen door and guided Angela in first, then he took a deep breath and walked in.

"Please introduce us," his mother said.

Dillon came inside as well, to watch what drama might unfold.

"Mother, I want you to meet," he hesitated a second. "Well, you're not the only Mrs. Chang in the family now."

The older Mrs. Chang looked at her son to see what he really meant. Then looking at Angela's warm smile, she knew it. "Oh, I'm so happy to meet you. Happy for both of you." She gave Angela a gentle, short hug. Looking at her son, she added, "She's so pretty."

"Thank you," Angela quietly said. She looked around the living room and saw a newspaper with two hands holding it by someone sitting on a giant easy chair behind it. Whoever it was seemed to be using the paper as a shield. It had to be Mr. Chang, the older.

"Dad," Chang said to the newspaper. "I came here to introduce you to my wife."

The newspaper lowered, revealing the older Mr. Chang's stern face.

"I know it's been a long time," Chang said, "so if we're not welcomed here, I understand, and we'll leave."

"No, need for that," Mrs. Chang said. "Your son is here," she said to her husband. "He's out of prison and married, so how about a welcome home for him?"

107

"He's been out for two or three years now," Mr. Chang said to her. "And now he finally comes home?"

"Allow him to explain," Mrs. Chang replied, "while I make some tea."

"Tea?" Mr. Chang said. He looked his wayward son over, then said. "Yes, I could use some."

Mrs. Chang turned to her new daughter-in-law. "How about helping me? I've got some other snacks we can serve as well."

Angela smiled. "Okay." She followed her into the kitchen.

"Father," Chang said, as he approached him with his hand extended.

Mr. Chang shook his hand, though weakly. "Sit down."

Chang sat down on the sofa facing him. His brother Dillon took a seat by the door.

His father looked past Chang into the kitchen to see his wife and Angela chatting quietly as they worked. "A little young for you, isn't she?"

"I never thought about that."

"The hell you didn't."

"Well, yeah, I considered it before we got married."

"Yes, I bet you did. Like a bulldog charging its mate."

"Isn't that how all marriages begin? Mom was ten years younger than you."

Mr. Chang glanced into the kitchen again and then back to his son. "Yeah. She still is." He reached over to a table near him and grabbed a long pipe and tobacco pouch. "So, what's the occasion? You finally coming around. Showing up without calling. Is it only to introduce us to your wife?"

"Something has come up where we might go away," Chang said quietly. "It might be the last opportunity to see you for a while. So I figured it was now or never and decided to take a chance."

Mrs. Chang entered the room and gently took the pipe out of her husband's hand. "We have guests," she said and walked back into the kitchen with it.

Mr. Chang gave a frustrated sigh. "So, you're going away? Where and why?"

"And good riddance for it," Dillon mumbled.

"We're going up north. We've got a little trouble and it might turn out badly."

"Trouble with the law?" Mr. Chang figured.

"No, it's not like that. In fact, I'm trying to protect the law against some terrorists. And it's about to become dangerous."

Mr. Chang stopped fiddling with the tobacco pouch and set it down. "I think you came here to tell me something. You're talking to me, but you're really not talking to me."

"All right," Chang said, leaning closer to his father. "Remember how you used to say that UFOs are real? Well, they are real, it seems, according to what I've been told and partially seen. And I might have to kill some bad people to prove that whoever or whatever is in those UFOs are infiltrating the business world."

Mr. Chang shook his head and smiled. "What a champion of the obvious you are. Of course, they're real. I haven't seen them, mind you, but I have it on authority from reliable elders who have. And they say that, whoever they are, are doing exactly as you suggest. I mean, what did you think they would do? Arrive in force with some kind of death ray and blow up our national monuments?"

"No, I know that's just for the comic books."

"Right. Just like the triads in China knew from the beginning, it's much more profitable to seduce, corrupt, intimidate and extort, than it is to murder."

2

"So, is this guy your brother?" Michaelson asked Emma showing her the photo from their surveillance camera the day of his one-man raid.

"Tell him what you told me," Elaine said, standing behind Michaelson. "It's important that he knows, now that we're planning this party."

"So, is this him?" Michaelson repeated, shaking the photo at her.

"Yeah. That's him," Emma said. A certified asshole. Like I told Ms. Elaine here, he just showed up out of the blue at my bar and slapped me around."

"Why did he do that?"

"Oh, he got angry about something I said."

"What did you say?" Michaelson pressed, squinting his eyes into lie detector mode.

Emma tried to control the fear that was growing inside her. Fear of banishment, more than the fear of punishment. Michaelson's group was her big opportunity in life. A lie could blow it for her. But so could the truth. "I was just talking about things I was doing."

"Such as?"

"Well, you see it's like this ..."

"You told him about us, didn't you?" Michaelson pushed.

"No, it wasn't like that. I didn't mention any names. Honest. In fact, he brought it up, like he knew all about this place."

"He knew about this place, all right," Michaelson said. "Came busting in her killing my men."

"I didn't know about that."

"Did you mention me or our group?"

"No, no. Not by name. Just that I was in a new business, that's all."

"I believe you for now," Michaelson said, relaxing his squint. "But you know what we do to anyone that breaks our trust."

"I would never break the trust. I had no idea what my brother was doing since he got out of prison. I hadn't seen him since he was locked up twelve years ago. I swear."

"No problem," Michaelson said, putting a clammy hand on her shoulder. He turned to Elaine. "But if he and that George are planning something, we'd better double our guards for the gathering."

"Yes, sir," Elaine said. "I've got a team of extra men standing by. Very professional. I'll bring them in."

"Your brother and two other guys killed two of our men in Chinatown yesterday. Did you know anything about that?"

"Nothing at all. We only talked a short time. He left my club in a hurry and I never saw or spoke to him after that."

"What I want to know is why your brother and his friends got off that boat and came back to the city."

"I don't know anything about his friends or a boat."

"All right," Michaelson said, satisfied for the moment. "But if he contacts you again, I want to hear about it right away. And I want you here for our gathering."

"I'd be honored sir."

Just then Judy, always wearing a red blouse, came in from the main entrance. "She's here. Her bus, or whatever you call it, is pulling up at the bottom of the driveway now."

"Good," Michaelson said. "By the way, Judy, this guy George you slept with. I know he's got guts, but is there anything more you can tell me about him?"

"Nothing much," Judy shrugged. "I let him pick me up at the marina, we went to a bar where he got into a fight. We went back to his place. I spent the night and left in the morning. That's about it."

"How was he in bed?" Elaine asked.

"He's a man. What else can I tell you?"

"Enough of this," Michaelson said. "Let's get outside and greet our benefactress."

The giant RV was just being shut off as Michaelson, Elaine and Judy stepped outside.

The RV door opened revealing Odina in the driver's seat. She stood up and stepped down to the ground, not acknowledging the three greeters. Next, Connie and Little Bird stepped down to the driveway. They stood next to Odina.

Michaelson unconsciously held his breath as he waited for his personal burning bush to appear and render her commandments.

It's been said that Cleopatra knew how to dress up in splendor to create a powerful image, so as to seduce and control her lowly subjects. Veronica had no such need. She achieved the same effect stepping down from the RV in jeans and a sleeveless tank top. Of course, the head of her doll that was sticking out of her bag, added to her already powerful image.

"Welcome back, Veronica," Michaelson said. "You have no idea what this means to me." He looked at the three Native American beauties attentively standing next to her. "And you brought some new friends, I see. Welcome, welcome."

Veronica looked at Elaine and Judy with indifference. "We've got some bags in there. Bring them in the house."

"We don't do that," Elaine said. "I'll get someone to ..."

Elaine was as tough as nails but couldn't stand up to Veronica's hammering stare. "Ah ... yeah ... sure ... we'll be glad to," She and Judy headed to the RV.

Veronica headed to the open door of the house, followed by her three friends and Michaelson. "You should give your help more training."

"Then they chased us down to the marina where George had a boat waiting," Chang explained to his father. "We cruised off, heading for Vancouver, but decided to come back here and get the goods on this Michaelson guy."

"You shouldn't have come back," Dillon said.

"This has nothing to do with you," his father retorted.

"No, what I mean," Dillon said, "is that it would have been safer for all of you to stay away from here. That's all."

Angela and Mrs. Chang came down from an upstairs, making the men stop talking.

"Now that you've shown her the house," Mr. Chang said to his wife, "why don't you show her what you've done with the garden."

Angela got the message. "Yes, I'd like to see it."

"It's quite something," Mr. Chang encouraged.

"Well," Mrs. Chang dutifully nodded. "Since it's a man's world, at least in this house, us women will leave you men to it." She motioned Angela to the back door, and they walked out of the living room.

"A man's world, she says," Mr. Chang grunted, "She's been bossing me around since you two and your sister were born. Never have children. Wives use them like bargaining chips."

"So what do you and your friends plan to do?" Dillon asked.

"They have no choice," Mr. Chang answered for his oldest son. "They have to find proof of what this group is doing."

"But speaking of my sister," Chang said. "There's a problem." He hesitated to think how to put it to his father and brother.

Mr. Chang raised a hand palm up. "What? Come on?"

"Well. Emma seems to be involved with them."

"Ai-ya," Mr. Chang breathed out.

"Why am I not surprised," Dillon said.

"You three were always wild," Mr. Chang sighed. "I had hopes for her, but I knew she'd end up in trouble. Haven't seen her for a couple of years."

Chang held his head down for a moment, then looked up at his father. "This place we plan to sneak into. It's going to be at one of their parties. Hopefully, we grab a laptop or download information, and then walk out. But if it goes bad, it'll become a firefight and there's a chance Emma will be there."

"Then you have to tell her to not be there," Mr. Chang said.

"I told her already. Told her to leave town. But I doubt she'll do that."

"Why wouldn't she leave?" Dillon asked.

"Because she has the hots for making big money with this group, is why." Chang said. "And I can't warn her again because it would put my wife's life on the line more than it already will be."

"What do you mean?" Mr. Chang asked.

"She'll be going to the party to get the goods on Michaelson."

"Going in alone?" Dillon asked.

"There'll be another guy as a date. They'll be three of us standing by with weapons if they get into trouble."

"Do you love this wife of yours?" Mr. Chang asked.

"As much as a guy like me can, I guess."

"What the hell kind of answer is that?"

"Yes, I do."

"She beautiful," Dillon said.

Chang looked at his brother in surprise. Dillon returned the look. Chang nodded slightly.

Mr. Chang leaned his head back into his chair. "Then, I guess, you have no choice, but to use her."

"But if she or the guy with her get caught, me and friends are going into that house shooting. Many will die. Hopefully, just the bodyguards."

"You said that everyone at the party is a terrorist. Is that right?" Dillon asked.

"Yes."

Dillon stood up thinking deeply. "Does that include the women?"

"According to my friend, it does. We were shot at by a woman that works for this Michaelson guy."

"Then you'll be forced to shoot women," Dillon said. "Any woman that might try to stop you."

"Right," Chang said. "I don't know if I can deal with that. I've hurt men that tried to hurt me. But I've never harmed a woman or a child."

Mr. Chang stood up and started slowly to pace back and forth. "All my life I've studied herbal medicine and acupuncture. Dedicated my life to easing people's pain. So, if everyone in the house are terrorists ..."

"Then?" Chang asked.

"Then, anyone that raises a pistol against you or your wife, shoot the bastard."

Chang stood up and looked at his father. "And if Emma's there?"

The two Mrs. Changs came back from the garden to see the three men standing wordless in the middle of the room.

CHAPTER 14

1

"You got the text to me set up?" George asked.

"One both phones ready to go," Angela said. "I hit the send button, you get the 'Take Action' message and you guys take action. Simple."

"Let's hope is doesn't come to that," Chang said.

"We just might get lucky and bring home the bacon," Miles said. "I've got the same message up and ready to send on my phone, too. But just my one phone. No back up."

"They didn't take my phone at the party I was at," George said. "I think you'll be alright."

Cathy entered the cabin. "The Uber car is here, and another man just drove up. I think he's for you, Mr. Chang."

"What?" Chang walked out of the cabin and saw a white Lincoln Town Car with an unknown brown-haired driver. Obviously, the Uber car. On the other side of the Lincoln, having just parked, Chang saw Dillon getting out of a car. "What are you doing here?"

"Dad sent me and also ..." Dillon looked around at the cabins and the Lincoln, and then started walking towards Chang.

"Also, what?"

"You need me."

"I do?"

"Yeah," Dillon said. "I've got more street smarts than you."

"Says you."

"Yeah, says me, saying that I never got caught and sent to prison."

"But that doesn't make you more street smart."

"A debatable point," Dillon said. "But a good subject for a conversation over a couple of beers."

"We've got root beer."

"Good enough," Dillon said stopping in front of Chang. "You got a weapon and lots of ammo for me?"

"Hey," the Uber driver called out. "I'm here for Angela."

115

"They'll be out soon," Chang said. He looked at Dillon and nodded his approval. "We'll have to make those beers for later."

"In that case," Dillon said, "they can be real beers."

"Sure thing. We'll get you holstered up in a minute. I have to see our infiltration team off."

"Sure."

Chang turned towards George's cabin. "Let's go."

"I'm coming," Miles called back.

Angela walked out from her and Chang's cabin. Chang walked over to meet her. She was wearing the same dress she wore to meet his parents. For this occasion, her long black hair was tied in a ponytail so as not to get in the way of bending over a computer or making a run for it.

"How do I look?" she asked Chang. "Do you think I'll pass for a party guest?"

"You're good."

"Don't knock yourself out with too many compliments."

"You look nice."

"Thank you."

"Now remember," Chang said, "once you get to Seattle, have your driver cruise around, so you can time it to get there not earlier ..."

"Not earlier than 2:30," she jumped in. "We've been over this twenty times."

"I know. But listen. We won't be in place till 2:15 so 2:30, okay? So no earlier than 2:30."

"Right."

"Well," came Miles' voice as he, George and Cathy came out of the cabin. "I've always wondered what *Uber Black* was. It's sure not the color of the car."

"Good, Miles. Keep 'em coming," George said.

"Let me check you out one more time," Cathy said to Miles. She looked over his black jacket and tie, then brushed his shoulders with her hands. "Okay, you'll pass."

"That's what I'm afraid of," Miles half-joked. "Passing the front door check and actually getting inside. Because that's when we really put it on the line."

"Good luck," George said as Miles headed for the Lincoln.

Miles went into a Bert Lahr voice, "Just one thing. Talk me out of it."

"Come on, Miles," George said. "Quit screwing around. Be serious."

"If I get serious, I won't make it through this."

"You'll make it," George said. "We'll all make it."

Dillon eyed Miles. *He doesn't look like the type of guy to handle this kind of job,* he thought.

Angela and Chang approached the car. Miles opened the back door. "Ladies first, my dear."

"Miles," Chang said, "This is my brother Dillon. He'll be part of the rescue team if needed. Just so you know."

Yeah,"Dillon said."Don't go shooting me or anything."

"Thanks for helping us, Dillon," Miles said.

"Yeah, sure."

Angela stuck her head in the car, but then stopped, turned and stepped back to Chang. She looked at him and then gave him gentle a hug with her head on his chest. "Just in case," she said quietly. She stepped back to see him nod to her. She smiled and then got into the car.

As Miles closed the door and went around to the other side to get in, Chang told the driver. "That party that they're attending is not till 2:30, so don't arrive before then."

"Sure thing," the driver said.

Chang could see Angela in the car shaking her head with a slight smile. The Lincoln backed up, turned toward the entrance, and drove out. Chang, George and Dillon watched it disappear down the road.

Cathy started up the eight-passenger SUV.

Now that Miles and Angela were on their way and Cathy was ready to drive them to Michaelson's neighborhood, George could address the obvious. "So, where's your friend, Gomez?" he asked Chang.

"He said he was coming for sure."

George put his hand on his hips. "Well, maybe after what happened in Chinatown, he got cold feet."

"I don't think so," Chang said. "Not Gomez."

"Maybe he figured the police would be on us by now," George speculated.

Chang shrugged. "Maybe so. I guess with his daughter and all he just ..."

"So you think he just took off with the money."

"He took the money to give to his daughter. The rest, I don't know."

"Well, I'm here to take his place," Dillon said. "And I'm just as good as anyone when it comes to street work."

"You are," Chang said.

"I guess we've got no choice," George said. "The three of us will have to handle it."

117

"Come on, Dillon," Chang said. "The weapons are in the SUV." The three men headed towards just as Gomez' car turned into the motel driveway.

He quickly parked, jumped out and trotted over to the three men about to get in the SUV. "Let's get this fiesta started," Gomez said, jumping in. The other three men followed.

"That's Cathy," Chang told Gomez pointing at her as she started up the engine.

"Hey, Cathy, Gomez said."How's your driving?"

"I'm sure it's a good as your shooting," she said without looking back.

"Good enough," Gomez said.

"This is my brother Dillon," Chang said. "Dillon, Gomez."

"How's it goin'? Dillon said.

"Hey, Dillon." Gomez said. "Okay, gun and ammo?" he asked Chang.

"I thought you grabbed a gun when we left you off after Chinatown," George said.

"I put it back in the bag," Gomez said. "I didn't want to take it to my daughter's house or get pick up packing."

"How was it with your daughter?" Chang asked.

"Very good," Gomez said. "Money's a great healer." He nodded at Chang, thought a moment, then said, "Weapon me up."

"In the bag," Chang said. "There's plenty of ammo, too. And get into a vest."

"Anybody forget anything?" Cathy asked.

"Put it in drive," George said.

"I'm keeping the gathering at no longer than two hours," Michaelson instructed Elaine. "I'll say a few words, then introduce Veronica."

"How long is she going to talk, Mr. M?"

"I don't know. She might make a speech or just say a few words. So be on your toes for whatever she wants to do."

"Right."

"As for me," Michaelson continued, "after Veronica finishes, I'll go through the crowd as usual, talk to a few people, then head downstairs. At the ninety-minute mark, start encouraging people to leave. And I mean everyone, including the new bodyguards."

"Got it," Elaine nodded. "I'll pass the word to Lyedecker and Veretti. Is the senator coming?"

"Of course. He knows Veronica is here and won't miss it for anything. But most of our group don't know about her being here, so it's going to be a big surprise for them."

"Some still don't believe she's real," Elaine added.

Michaelson looked around at the caterers who were setting up the food and drink tables. "Well, anyone that comes today will start believing in her."

"What about her three friends?"

"What about them?"

"Are they supposed to talk, work the crowd, or what? The less surprises the better."

"She might introduce them. She might not. For this gathering, it's just a matter of keeping Veronica happy, keeping security tight, and give our guests their first look at our celestial princess."

"And the senator?" Elaine asked.

"He likes to be on his own, so I'll just introduce him to Veronica and then let him do his thing."

"Yeah, dragging 'em off to a room, two at a time."

Michaelson looked around. "Our men are here, but where's the new security men you arranged?" Elaine looked at her watch. "They should be arriving soon."

"About how many?"

"I ordered a baker's half-dozen. That'll discourage any outsiders, including George and that Chang guy. Though I can't think of a reason they'd want to come here now. Especially after Chinatown. They must know we're on guard now."

"I'm sure they left town after they got their personal belongings or whatever they came back for," Michaelson surmised. "Especially after leaving the bodies of our men there. The police will be after them now, for sure."

"Good riddance," Elaine said. She looked down the long hallway to see Veronica and her three friends approaching. Elaine had been intimate with powerful men and stunning women, but had never seen such a blend of power and striking beauty in one person.

"How long till the gathering?" Veronica asked Michaelson as she approached.

Michaelson's face began to redden with trepidation. "Oh, another ninety minutes. I always demand that my quests are punctual."

"How are you able to control that?" she asked.

"Elaine here, is our disciplinarian."

Veronica took a quick glance at Elaine's serious face and muscular body that was giving her sleeveless pants suit a good stretch. "Yes, I can see that. You'll have to show me what techniques you use some time."

Elaine bowed her head slightly. "Gladly. Anytime." Then she eyed Veronica's three companions like a malnourished gambler at a Vegas buffet, zeroing in on Little Bird.

Veronica noticed Elaine's interest in her friends and contemplated feeding Elaine to them after the party. And maybe having a bite herself. She turned back to Michaelson. "How many of our kind are we now in Seattle?"

Michaelson wanted to wipe his brow but didn't as he knew Veronica abhorred weakness. "Nearing three hundred now. Of course, we never have more than a hundred at any one time to our gatherings here. But our senator is coming, and I can tell you that he's extremely excited to meet you." He looked are her three companions standing behind her. Little Bird was looking at him with untrustful eyes. "I mean to say, he'll be excited to meet all of you."

That did nothing to change Little Bird's expression.

"Have our dresses arrived?" Veronica asked.

"Yes, of course. I ordered them days ago when you called. They're downstairs. I'll show you where we have them." Michaelson held his hand out toward the descending stairs.

Veronica turned and headed there with her disciples behind her. Before following, Michaelson quickly grabbed the handkerchief in his breast pocket and gave his forehead a quick dab, replaced it and turned to follow the four women.

"Are you okay, Mr. M?" Elaine asked as he was walking away.

"Fine. Fine," he said descending the stairs.

Elaine turned toward the double front doors. She walked over to the large man standing there holding a metal detecting wand. "How's it going, Freddie?"

"The wand is all charged up and ready, ma'am," he said making a fist.

"Take it easy big fella. This isn't WrestleMania. But I like your style."

"Sure thing, ma'am. I wish I had made it to WrestleMania."

"There was nothing wrong with *Channel Two Wrestling Night*."

"Ah, those bums never let me win."

"So look, Freddie," Elaine said. "If the wand does buzz, have one of the other men check the guest out. It's probably just a watch or pen or something, not a bazooka. Right? So no airplane-spinning them to the mat, huh?"

The once local gladiator Freddie-the-Smasher gave a girlish giggle. "That's funny ma'am. Right. No airplane-spins."

"Who's watching the cell phone boxes?"

"Just me, ma'am. I can handle both."

"No, I'll get someone. You tend to the invitations and scanning. And where the hell's those security guys I ordered from Newcastle?"

"I don't know who they are, but there's a bunch of big guys in suits that's been standing out there for a while."

"Well, bugger me blind," Elaine complained as she opened the front door. "Why didn't you tell me?"

"I just make sure people that come throu ..."

"Yeah, all right," she interrupted as she went outside. She walked over the group of six men in the driveway who were chatting, with a couple of them smoking. "Hey, are you guys from Newcastle Security?"

A broad shoulder, handsome man, most likely the team leader, turned toward her. "Yes, we are. And ready to go."

Elaine shook her head. "Then why weren't you ready enough to ring the damned doorbell and let me know you're here?"

The men stopped chatting. Two of them tossed down their cigarettes to the pavement and snuffed them out with their shoes.

Elaine hated black stains on the driveway, but before she could remark on it, the team leader took a powerful step toward her. "Look," he said. "We're an hour early and we just got here. Now if that's all right with you, then I'm Martin Cavanaugh. I'm in charge of these men. And if it's not all right, we can trot back down the hill to our cars and leave."

Elaine controlled her annoyance back to professionalism. "Fine. Fine. I'm Elaine. I'm in charge of house security."

"Sure. We talked on the phone."

Elaine looked them over. "Okay, there's six of you. Fine."

"We've got one more with a dog down the hill," Cavanaugh said. "A baker's half dozen, including me. Exactly as you ordered."

"I like that," Elaine said giving him a slight smile. "Forget the doorbell remark."

"Where do you want us?"

She turned and looked at the house. "Let's see, I've got Hobbs and Costa taking care of the downstairs. Lyedecker and Veretti upstairs, with Freddie at the door. Let's say, one of your men out here at the front door. He can handle the phone box as well. One in the living room. One in upper hallway by the bathroom. Two on the upper balcony that runs the length of the house. They'll be able to control the grounds at the back. And keep your dog man down at the bottom of the driveway. That's six. Right?"

"Right."

"Good," she nodded, adjusting her stance to show off her thin waistline. "And I want you with me in the living room."

"All right."

"Are all of your men heeled."

"Yes," Cavanaugh smiled. "If we're in a Bogart movie, we would be considered *heeled*."

Elaine returned his smile. "Are you as good as you look?"

Cavanaugh quit smiling. "No client has ever asked for a refund."

"Does that include women?"

"Okay, I'll disperse my men," he said ignoring, but heeding her remark.

"Stick around after the party."

"I always do for billing purposes."

"Good," Elaine said, heading back inside. "Join me in the living room once your men are positioned."

Cavanaugh thought he heard her say something like *other positions,* as she walked away. But he wasn't sure.

Back in the living room, Elaine approached Lyedecker and Veretti. "I want you two to stay in this room. Keep a general eye on the crowd, especially when Mr. M and that Veronica speak, if she speaks."

"Are those four women going to be staying here awhile?" Lyedecker wanted to know.

"Why?" Elaine smiled. "Have you got designs on one of them?"

"I'm a professional, Elaine. You know that. My interest in them is purely for security purposes."

"Purely monetary, he means," Veretti added.

"That too," Lyedecker said.

"But for me," Veretti said, "I wouldn't mind getting to know those four better."

"Oh, yeah?" Elaine responded. "Well, for today, keep it professional. We've got a bigger crowd than usual invited, so stay loose, the both of you."

"Yes, ma'am," Veretti said.

Elaine turned to go downstairs. "And hands off the one they call Little Bird."

CHAPTER 15

1

1:55PM: Cathy pulled the SUV to a dead-end street that had access to a tree infested hill that would lead George, Chang, Dillon and Gomez in a semi-circular path to another wooded hill that overlooked the back of Michaelson's house. Once there, they would stand by, hidden from view. If needed, they could work their way to Michaelson's back yard area in under two minutes. If not needed, they would work their way back to the drop off point and call Cathy for pick-up.

Not to look like a four-man invasion unit, they got out of the SUV slowly, with their weapons and bullet-proof-vests hidden under casual clothes. Once four pairs of feet hit the asphalt, Cathy hit the automatic door button and slowly drove off as it closed. She headed to what would be the extraction point, should the team have to go in.

Otherwise, and hopefully for all concerned, Miles and Angela would be able to get the data they needed and leave Michaelson's house with the rest of the party-goes. Just another good-looking, mildly inebriated couple with enough data to shut down the invasion of earth.

The four men hit the grassy dirt that headed up the hill and into the dense tree area. The only houses on that dead-end street were seventy-five yards away. So, they figured that no tell-tale housewife, who should be watching *The Bold and the Beautiful*, instead of looking out her window, would see and report them.

George took the lead up the hill, followed by Gomez. Chang and Dillion walked side by side.

"Say is the Red Dragon Lantern still there?" Chang asked his brother as they got closer to the cover of the trees.

"It's still there," Dillon said.

"Do mom and dad still eat there on Friday nights?"

"Not for a while."

"After this is over, how about we take them there for some *gu-lo-yook-fawn*?" Chang asked.

"They'd like that."

"Does Danny Ming still work there?"

"Nah, he died."

"Ah, too bad," Chang said sincerely. "I liked him."

"Me, too."

"Lousy cook."

2

2:27 p.m. Miles figured in another five or six minutes, the Uber driver would get them to Michaelson's house. He was sitting in the back seat of the Lincoln with Angela. They hadn't spoken much since leaving the cabins. But now, the reality of what they were attempting, began to sink into them. Especially Miles.

"My ex-boss," Miles said to Angela, "this guy, Raskin. He's kind of a western aficionado. He collects cowboy and horse statues. You know, John Wayne posters with slogans and stuff like that."

"Yeah? So?" Angela said.

"Well, before going into some sales presentations, where he felt like he was in over his head, he would often say; 'I feel like I'm walking into the O.K. Corral'."

"Uh-huh. So?"

"So, I feel like I'm riding into the damned O.K Corral."

"You're not the only one riding in."

"I know that. I just feel like I'm heading for my last roundup."

"Don't talk like that," she said. "All we have to do..."

Miles put a finger to his lips and tilted his head towards the driver who was looking at them in his rear-view mirror.

Angela nodded. "All we have to do is get some oats for our horses, dance a couple of jigs, and join the wagon train west."

"If not, ..." Miles thought for a second.

"Yeah?"

"If not, let's hope Earp, his brothers and Doc will help us get the hell out of Dodge."

Finally, the Uber driver couldn't control his curiosity. "Say are you guys in one of those live western shows or something?"

"Yeah, exactly," Miles said pointing to Angela. "Meet Annie Oakley."

2:37p.m. The Lincoln carrying Miles and Angela approached Michaelson's circular driveway that had a line of luxury cars moving around it, dropping off guests. Angela nudged Miles with her elbow and tilted her head to her side of the car. Miles looked out the window and saw a man standing at the bottom of the driveway with a German Shepard. Miles raised the palm of his hands in a 'nothing we can do about it' gesture.

Seeing they were fifth back of a line of cars and that the other quests getting out of their cars before they got to the front, Miles pulled out a twenty, handed it to the driver, "Thanks for the tour, buddy. We'll get out here."

"Sure. And good luck with your show."

"Thanks, we'll need it," Miles said as he opened the door, got out and helped Angela out. Angela took his arm as they walked toward the entrance of the large house. They looked at the other arriving guest, mostly beautiful women, done up for the afternoon party. "I guess they're having a beauty contest today," he joked to Angela, just to make conversation and look like real guests.

Angela took the cue. "Yes, it looks that way. I'm glad I'm not entered, I wouldn't even place."

"You'd take the gold for sure. And I mean that."

"I wasn't fishing."

"I wish that I was fishing right now. At a lake far away from this place," he said as they reached the open doorway.

"Put your cell phones in a slot and take the number tag," the guard by the open door ordered.

Miles and Angela complied. *Well, there goes those phones*, Miles thought. He and Angela then followed the line of guests into the foyer.

"Invitation please," they heard the guard with the wand ask the couple in front of them. The woman pulled out a white invitation card from her purse and showed it to the guard.

"Oh, Jesus," Miles whispered to Angela. "What's wrong with that Cathy? Didn't she hear anything about invitations in three days of monitoring their calls?"

"We couldn't have gotten one even if we had known about it," Angela whispered back.

The couple ahead of them, moved into the large marble foyer. The guard looked at Angela and Miles. "Invitation, please."

"You know," Miles said to Angela, "before going in, I need a smoke. Let me have a few puffs before ..."

"Oh, I know you," Angela said to the guard.

Miles looked at her and then the guard. *What's she trying to pull?* he thought. *Better to fake a smoke break and get out of here.*

"You know me?" the guard questioned with a broken tooth smile.

Whatever she's trying to pull off, it isn't going to work, Miles feared.

"The Masher, right?" Angela smiled and put a hand on the guard's arm for good measure.

"It's Smasher," he happily corrected. "That's me. Freddie-the-Smasher."

"Sure," Angela said feigning excitement. "I watched you all the time on TV. You were really wild and strong." She put her other hand on his arm.

"Yeah, those were the days."

He's buying it, Miles thought, forcing a smile as he watched Angela pulling out all the stops.

"Well, I know your busy," she said to Freddie, "but I hope we can talk later."

"Sure," Freddie said. "Yeah, sometime during the party, I'll have a little time."

"That'll be great," she said, taking a step forward, with Miles about to follow.

"Oh." He stopped her with his large hand on her arm. "Invitation, please."

Angela stopped. "Of course." She opened her purse and looked in. "Oh, I remember. I put it on the car seat. Miles, go after our driver before he leaves."

"Right," Miles said, turning toward the driveway, pretending to look for their car.

"Oh, forget it," Freddie said. He turned to the next couple. "Invitation please."

Miles didn't hesitate. He stepped up closer to Angela, took her arm and guided her toward the living room. "I'm sure glad you watch wresting," Miles whispered.

"My father had charge of the remote," she whispered back. "so I watched what he watched. I'll have to thank him for it if we get out of this."

"When we get out of this," Miles corrected.

"When did you get so positive?"

"Just now when we got past that guy with no invitation and no scanning."

"My real phone wouldn't have shown up on that little scanner anyhow. It's turned off, triple wrapped with that stuff, and hidden where no one would dare scan or frisk."

"Where's that?" Miles asked just to keep his mind off the danger and not expecting an answer.

She didn't give him one.

"Let's find a restroom, so you can turn it on," Miles said. "I'll feel more relaxed to know we're connected to the calvary."

"We won't need them. With this many people and more coming in, we can blend in, get the job done and leave."

They entered the living room which already had about sixty guests in there, drinking, chatting, and grabbing snacks off trays carried around by servers. It looked to be about 75% women, all beautiful. Standing in the middle of five of them was a tall, handsome, grey-hair man in his 60s. Angela also recognized him from TV. Not a wrestler, but a senator.

Miles grabbed two glasses of champagne from a server and handed one to Angela. "Here's to the thumb drive in my pocket," he toasted quietly. "May it get filled with tons of incriminating evidence."

Angela held up her glass and took a tiny sip.

"That's right," Miles said. "These are just props to help us blend in. We can get blind drunk later."

"I don't drink. Hence the token sip."

"While the guests are still arriving," Miles said looking around. "Let's see how far we can wander around and maybe find a computer or two while looking for the bathroom."

"Take my hand and lead me."

"Proud to."

They walked away from the crowded living room and down a large hall. They passed one room and looked in to see three women and one man talking surrounded by shelves of books. Two of the women looked at Miles and Angela as they slowly passed by. Angela smiled and nodded. They returned it.

Moving down the hall one women came out of a room with a security man standing next to it. "Is this the restroom?" Angela asked the woman.

"Yes, right in there."

"I'll just be a minute," Angela told Miles.

"Sure."

She went in and closed the door leaving Miles eye to eye with the security man. Miles nodded. The man stood motionless. "Did you ever know a woman to just take just a minute?" he smiled at the man.

"I wouldn't know, sir," the man said.

Jesus, what an asshole. Miles looked down the hall to see a beautiful woman in a white taffeta dress approaching. "Hello," he said as she passed by.

"Hello," she responded as she continued to the living room.

Wow. If they all look as good as her, maybe I'll ditch Angela and join the club, he thought to amuse away his fears.

Miles looked at the ceiling, then his shoes, then turned and casually walked down the hall to look around as he waited for Angela.

He saw another room that had its door open. He walked over to it, under the eye of the security man, and looked in. It was just a bedroom where a ravishing woman was using a wall mirror to put on some lipstick. "Hey, what the hell?" a middle-aged man said appearing at the door from the blind side of the room.

"Oh, sorry," Miles said. "The door was open. I'm just waiting for my girlfriend."

"Well, that's okay, buddy," the man said, changing his tone. "Did Michaelson show up, yet?"

"Ah, I just arrived, but there's nothing special going on yet, I don't think."

"Cool," the man said. "I'll see you around."

"Sure." Miles slowly walked back to the restroom door. "Quite a place," he said to the security man who made no response.

Finally, Angela came out. "Thank you for waiting."

Miles smiled and pointed down the hall. "Nothing's happening, yet. Let's see who else is here today," he said for the sake of the guard.

Angela took Miles' arm and they started slowly strolling down the hall. "Okay," she whispered. "My phone's on. Got the text up with no shut off timer. All I have to do is press 'send'."

"Good," Miles breathed out as they walked. "Be careful not to butt-dial it. We don't want our friends to crash the party unless we really need them."

"Don't worry about it."

"Well, it's just that my girlfriend often butt-dials me. And considering she's still has a rotary phone, she's very talented."

Angela kept a straight face and voice. "You're funny, Miles. Once we get to the boat, remind me to laugh."

"Thank you."

They came to the end of the hall where there were three doors. One open and two closed. Miles looked back down the hall to check the security man. He was looking toward the living room, so he quickly grabbed the doorknob of one of them to take a quick look. It was locked.

They looked into the open door. A large bedroom. No desk, no computer. Miles looked at the security man down the hall. Now he was talking to two women.

"This is our chance," he said to Angela. He grabbed the doorknob of the other room. It opened. A quick look inside showed it to be some kind of multi-purpose storage room. File cabinets, shelves of food, blankets, tables, exercise bike, weights, cardboard boxes and several curious looking wooden boxes. But no computer.

Miles turned to see the guard had finished talking to the women and was walking toward them. *We're screwed.*

Angela saw the panic on Miles' face. "What?"

Miles put his hand on the back of her head, puckered his lips and moved into her. Knowing what he was going for, she guided his head to the side of her's and wrapped her arms around him. "Work my neck all you want," she whispered, "but not my lips."

"I love it when you talk dirty," he nervously whispered as he kept his ears opened for the guard's footsteps. He continued kissing her neck, moving his hands around her back to sell the love scene to the danger bearing down on them. Finally, he asked, "What's happening."

"He's going back," she said.

Miles backed off of her. "Sorry. It's the only thing I could think of."

"Don't worry. You did good," she said seriously as she reached in her purse, pulled out a handkerchief and dried her neck.

"George said, when he was here, Michaelson came up from the lower floor. So that's probably where he has his important stuff."

"Looks that way." She placed her handkerchief back in her purse.

"Let's stroll back to the living room, casual like."

"Right."

They moved down the hall, passed the *asshole* security man and entered the living room that was more crowded than before. A young woman in a black silk gown was gently playing Litszt's *Love Dream* on the piano.

The senator was still talking with the women. But when he noticed the Asian beauty entering the room with Miles, his concentration broke from them. "Excuse me," he said turning and zeroing his attention on *fresh meat* as he called newcomers.

Approaching Angela, he held out his hand. "Good afternoon. I'm Senator Andrews."

She extended her hand and let him take it. "Hello. I'm Angela."

"So nice to meet you, Angela."

"And this is my friend Miles."

Andrews shook Miles' hand. "Good to meet you, Miles. Democrat or Republican?"

Miles smiled trying to select the right answer. "Well, you see, I'm always trying to ... I mean ..."

Andrews laughed. "I'm just messing with you. For world domination, bipartisanship is the name of the game."

"Right," Miles patronized.

Andrews turned to Angela. "Speaking about domination. How do you feel about it?"

This house is filled with assholes, Miles thought.

"Well Senator," Angela started to give herself time to think, "I guess it depends on the political party and who's doing the dominating."

Andrews chuckled. "Great answer, little lady. I'll have to remember that one."

Angela gave Andrews a slight smile.

"She's been dominating me ever since we started dating," Miles said humorously, to imply his ownership of Angela. *Now I'm the asshole*, he thought.

"Been dominating you?" Andrews chuckled again. "You two are the *Sonny and Cher* of our congregation. You should work on some routines to entertain at our parties."

"Thank you, Senator," Angela indulged him.

Andrews winked at her and said, "And maybe I could entertain you with some routines I think you'd enjoy, little lady."

With that as an exit line, Andrews turned and went back to the women he'd been talking to.

"What the fuck?" Miles whispered to himself.

"I'm starting to agree with my husband," Angela said.

"About what?"

"Buying some explosives and blowing this place up."

"Ladies and gentlemen," came a loud female voice. The crowd's chatter subsided. "Thank you for coming on this special day."

Miles and Angela looked to see Elaine standing in front of the stairway that lead down to the lower floor. "Here's our host. Mr. Henry Michaelson."

The crowd applauded, some cheered, and one man whistled as Michaelson slowly ascended the stairs up to the living room into everyone's view.

The devil himself, rising from hell below, Miles thought. *Well, ain't he the one.*

132

Michaelson wore a dark suit with a blue tie and a smug expression. He looked over the crowd of beautiful women and well-dressed men like he had the power to bestow sainthood.

"Yes," he said loudly to the group, "And a very special day it is indeed." He paused for effect, then continued. "I'm sure most of you have heard the story of a little Native American girl from Arizona who was touched by a great power from above. Some people believed. Some thought it a mere myth that we use to recruit members. Whether you believed or not, we know most of you women joined for the financial rewards. Most of you men, well, we know what you joined for."

Men in the group chuckled and nodded. Many of the women giggled. Emma, standing in the center of the group, called out, "We know the reason," causing others to snicker. Michaelson joined in with a chuckle.

Miles and Angela stood among them feeling like undercover Christians at a Caligula orgy.

"Well, be that as it may," Michaelson continued, "as long as you contribute to the growth and prosperity of all, we don't care why you joined."

"Just keep giving us those stock tips," Senator Andrews called out. "I love selling short and collecting tall."

The crowd cheered. Some started chanting "Short, short, short", then stopped when Michaelson raised his hands with a smile.

"Don't worry," Michaelson assured them. "Our financial consultants are always searching for unstable companies."

So you can give the green light to your bombmakers, Miles thought.

"Now," Michaelson said, "back to the reason we're meeting today. Back to that myth, as some of you say. Well, I am her to tell you, that myth has just arrived here. She's been here twice in the past for private meetings with me. But this is the first time she's appeared at one of our gatherings. Ladies and gentlemen, the future is indeed now and indeed here."

Man. P.T. Barnum would be proud of this guy. Miles stopped himself from rolling his eyes. *Who is he introducing? Tiny Tim?*

"So, without further ado, I give you Veronica."

The group went into pin-drop mode. Miles half-expected a flurry of trumpets. But nothing happened. A long 30 seconds went by. Some in the group began to quietly mumble. Miles heard one woman, under her breath say, "I guess she really is a myth."

In the back of the room, Veretti whispered to Lyedecker, "Want me to go downstairs to see if there's a problem."

Lyedecker looked at Michaelson across the room. He didn't seem worried. "Hold on a bit."

Then the sound of feet from below on the stairway could be heard. In a few seconds, long, black hair came into view. One more step up and the crowd could see the face of a beautiful Native American woman. The crowd applauded, but slowly stopped when Michaelson's hand gently came up. The woman came around the stair railing and stood behind Michaelson keeping a serious demeanor.

Another set of feet could be heard ascending. Another long black-haired beauty appeared, moved around the railing, stopping next to the first woman.

Some of the crowd gave each other looks, but no one dared to make a sound and interrupt Michaelson's obviously planned procession.

Jesus, Miles thought. *If this keeps up, it'll take on all the trappings of a third-grade production of Peter Pan.*

Another dark-haired beauty ascended and took her place next to the first two.

The women in the crowd, excluding Angela, instead of wondering which one was Veronica, were thinking about what kind of competition each of the three women would be for them. The men in the crowd, including Miles, were judging which of the three women they would like to start with first.

"Ladies and gentlemen," Michaelson said, "from left to right; Connie Hawkins, Odina Maskwa and Little Bird Harjo."

"Elaine's next squeeze," Veretti whispered to Lyedecker who kept a straight face.

The audience gave a perfunctory, gentle applause as Veronica's maids-in-waiting seemed to be looking past them as if they didn't exist. Arrogance to the point of not caring one way or the other about anybody.

Though this pageant seemed ridiculous on the surface to Miles, something very wrong seemed to be happening. His Greek mythology kicked in; *There they stand; the three heads of Cerberus. The tri-headed dog that guards the gates of the underworld. Next up, what? The overlord, no doubt.*

Angela could feel it, too. She hadn't had such nightmarish feelings since that foggy Chinatown night when she had been attacked. On that night, her future husband arrived in time to save her. Would he arrive in time now, if needed?

Another sound of feet on the stairs broke the stillness in the room. In a few seconds, Veronica rose into the living room wearing a purple satin dress that hugged the voluptuous curves of her dark-skinned body.

She gave off such an air of grander that her beholders could only manage a smattering of applause.

What? Miles thought. *I know her. The girl in San Francisco that gave George her number.*

Miles looked at Angela, wanting to say something about it, but the room was too quiet. *What's with that doll?* he asked himself. *I remember she was carrying it at the convention.*

Veronica nodded to Michaelson who couldn't control a Cheshire Cat grin. She turned to her followers and smiled. "The future is now," she said.

The room broke into cheers.

When the room got quiet again, Veronica said, "Money, relationships, health, possessions. None of that matters without the one true ingredient to sustain life, power. Power to take from others, that which they would take from you if showing weakness." She paused and seemed to look over each person in the room. "And I don't see a weak one among you." She looked at Michaelson and nodded a 'good job of recruiting' to him. He nodded back a 'thank you'.

"It says in your bible," she continued, "'You shall receive power when the holy spirit has come upon you. And I have arrived to tell you, that the end of the earth has come for those who are weak. And the powerful shall inherit the earth."

As she continued mesmerizing the group with a mixture of religion, wealth, politics, potentiality, and sensual awards for the loyal, Miles eyed the stairway entrance that lead to the lower floor. That's where the five actors of this badly written play of the absurd had entered from. And that had to be where Michaelson's office was, as George had suggested.

Miles tapped Angela on the arm and gave a slight motion to the stairway entrance. She looked and then blinked her understanding to him. *But how to get down there?* He contemplated.

Veronica finished her oration with, "The end of things is at hand; therefore, be self-controlled for the sake of your power. Above all, keep loving one another earnestly, as each of you has received a gift of glory and dominion forever."

Miles half-expected an amen from the group, but instead they broke wildly into applause as Veronica took a few steps back to stand next to her Arizona partners-in-power.

Michaelson took a step forward. "All right. You're free to eat, drink and chat. And don't worry, Veronica and I will join you for a while. So, enjoy."

The enlightened members gradually started up conversations as they went to the food table. Veronica and Michaelson moved into the crowd to further enjoy all the adulation.

"This is our chance," Miles whispered to Angela. Grab a plate of food and meet me there by the stairs."

She nodded and moved toward the food table.

Miles moved through the crowd, still with the drink in his hand. He smiled and nodded to people as arrived at the stairway. Soon, Angela walked up to him, dinner plate in hand.

"Well," he said to her. "No paper plates and plastic forks for this shindig, I see."

"First class all the way."

"Would you like to see if there's a quiet place downstairs to sit down and eat?"

"Seems like a good idea," Angela said as they turned toward the stairs.

"Hello again, miss," a high, gruff voice came from behind them.

They turned to see Freddie, wand in hand. "Oh, hello again, Mr. Smasher," Angela said. "That was an exciting speech, wasn't it?"

"I wasn't really listening," Freddie said. "Did you get all you wanted to eat?"

"Yes, I did. Thank you."

"That's good. I have to get back to the door, but I just wanted to remind you to come and talk when you have a chance."

"I sure will."

"Okay, great. See you soon." Freddie turned and went back to the door.

Miles smiled at Angela, quickly scanned the room to see if anyone was paying attention to them, and then motioned her to head downstairs. "You sure have a knack for soothing the savage beast," he said following her down.

"I hope I have a knack for getting out of here," she said as she reached the bottom of the stairs.

Miles reached the bottom to see that he and Angela were being looked at by a guard seated by the lower balcony window. Miles couldn't figure, if the guard was checking them out for security or just checking out Angela. "Here's a good place," Miles said to her pointing to a red leather sofa. They both sat down.

"Want any of this?" Angela said moving her plate towards him.

"No, thanks. I'll just finish my drink. You go ahead."

Angela began picking at her food. Miles saw the balcony guard slide open the glass door near the inside guard. "Hey, got a smoke?" Costa asked.

"Yeah," Hobbs said reaching into his jacket pocket. "I'll join you for a minute." He got up and went out to the balcony.

Miles waited till Costa and Hobbs had their backs to them as they leaned on the railing lighting cigarettes. Then he said to Angela, "Excuse me a minute. I'll look for a restroom."

She worriedly looked at Costa and Hobbs, still with their backs to them. "Sure."

Miles got up casually and walked down the empty hallway. The first room that he came to was on his left. He tried the doorknob. It turned and he opened the door. The room had spots of strong green light hitting various parts of the room caused by a spotlight hitting a disco-style mirrored ball that was hanging from the ceiling.

He also saw a small bar, stereo system, and curiously fifteen or so Japanese futons lying on the thick red carpeted floor. Miles surmised it was a private disco room that had been converted into a kind of group guest room. But he didn't know the half of it.

He quietly closed the door and turned to the room ahead and to the right. The knob on the door turned and he opened it. Bingo. Large oak desk, plush chair, file cabinets and most important the holy grail; two desktop computers and a laptop.

He looked down the hall to see Angela was watching him. Knowing that he could get the job done without her, he gave her the 'stay there' sign with the palm of his hand and entered, closing the door behind him.

He set his drink down and plopped into the overstuffed leather chair in front of the computers. Were his hands shaking with excitement or fear? he wondered. He was used to business pressure; calling up his talent at will to deliver on a deadline. But this deadline was deadly. It was time to focus under pressure, not fold.

Punching some keys on the computer that was nearest him, got him nothing but a photo of Veronica's famed meteor crater and a log in window. *No way*, he thought. He was a wiz with computers, but he was no hacker and besides, there was no time.

He moved to the next desktop. The same thing, only a photo of the Las Vegas train wreck, with the crashed Statue of Liberty replica lying next to it.

Screw this, he thought and grabbed the laptop. It was a light, 11-inch Macbook Air. He put it under his jacket, held it tight with his arm and headed for the door. He started to open it, but then stopped to turn back and grabbed his drink with his free hand. Now slowly he opened the door and took a drink to act like he was drunk and had stumbled into the wrong room. But he saw there was no one in the hall to perform for. Not ever Angela on the sofa. Only her lunch plate. *Where did she go to?*

He walked casually down the hall like he was just returning from a restroom. As he rounded the corner, Angela came into view. He could see her through the glass door, standing on the balcony with Costa and Hobbs. *Good girl. Keeping them distracted. Now what to do?*

He picked up her lunch plate and walked toward the open balcony door. He noticed Hobbs had his hand on Angela's back and it was slowly descending downward. She didn't object or move. She was playing her distraction act all the way.

"Hey, honey," Miles said, trying to sound slightly drunk. "Aren't you gonna finish your food?"

"Yeah. In a minute," she said harshly without turning around. "Can't you see I'm busy?"

Miles saw that neither Hobbs nor Costa paid him any mind. Costa was too busy watching Hobb's hand on Angela reach its firm, rounded goal and rest there, knowing that once seduced, he'd get his turn with her as was their habit of sharing. *What a couple of assholes*, Miles thought. *Right in front of me. Not caring if I'm the boyfriend, husband or what.*

"Ah, come on honey," Miles said in the best wimpy voice he could muster. Michaelson wants everyone to meet Veronica upstairs. He's probably wondering what's happened to us."

"No. Michaelson's wondering what the fuck you're doing down here," came Michaelson's voice behind him.

Hobbs, Costa and Angela quickly turned around and saw Michaelson and two of the Cavanaugh's bodyguards standing behind Miles.

Miles turned slowly, still staying in his drunk act. "We just came down her to eat in quiet," he said to Michaelson. "And then your two men here started putting their hands on my wife, so I figured ..."

"Shut up," Michaelson demanded. "We've got cameras all over here, including my office."

"Hey, sorry. I'm a little drunk and was just checking out the place. That's a...."

Michaelson slapped the plate out of Miles' hand, not caring about the mess it made. He yanked on Miles' other hand and the laptop fell to the floor.

"Okay." Miles shrugged making one last feeble excuse, "I need a new laptop, so ... you know. Go ahead and call the cops."

"Take him into my office," Michaelson ordered the two guards as he grabbed his laptop off the floor. "And you two Romeos out there," he yelled at Hobbs and Costa, "bring that bitch as well."

Hobbs grabbed Angela by the hair and neck as Elaine had trained all her guards in handling women and dragged Angela inside with Costa following.

"Get your hands off of me," Angela yelled.

"Shut the hell up," Hobbs growled at her, disappointed that their intimacy had come to an abrupt stop.

She grabbed his hand that was pulling her hair as they went into the hallway. "What's the matter?" she yelled, her street smarts kicking in. "Did you have enough of my ass?"

"I might get some of that ass, if this goes the way I think it will," Hobbs said. Costa joined in, grabbing the struggling Angela's shoulders as they continued down the hall.

Michaelson entered his office, followed by the guards holding Miles. Then Hobbs and Costa entered controlling Angela. Michaelson set his laptop down on his desk. "Well, judging from her looks," he said, pointing to Angela, "she's with that Chinatown convict Chang. And you," he said, pointing to Miles, "must be working with that traitor George."

Miles and Angela stood mute. They were smart enough to know that Michaelson was holding all the cards now.

"Get his wallet and grab her purse," Michaelson ordered.

Costa and Hobbs did what they were told. Costa handed Mile's wallet to Michaelson. "Empty her purse," he told Hobbs.

Hobbs complied and dumped the insides of Angela's purse onto the desk. Her phone thumped onto the glass top. Michaelson picked it up. "How did you get in here with this?"

"My secret," Angela said.

"Well, little miss 'my secret', you came in with it, but you and your friend here are not going out at all."

"What's happening?" Elaine asked, entering with Cavanaugh, the head of the Newcastle guards. They had been talking together in the living room when they got the word about something going on downstairs.

Michaelson picked up Angela's phone and held it under Elaine's nose. "And you shit-for-brains-chief-of-security, how did she get in here with this?"

"I don't know," Elaine said. "She probably had it up her ass. It happens."

"It's not supposed to happen here," Michaelson yelled.

"I'll call the police to pick her up," Cavanaugh said. "And I guess this one, too."

"No police," Elaine told him. "We like to handle our problems in house."

"What?" Cavanaugh asked.

"So, you're from Newcastle Security?" Michaelson asked Cavanaugh.

"Yeah," Elaine jumped in as Miles eyed Angela's phone on the desk. "He brought in six man. Good men."

"Well, he and his good men can go home now," Michaelson said.

"What kind of place is this?" Cavanaugh asked. "You're supposed to have the police handle these things."

"Just leave and bill me," Michaelson said.

Cavanaugh looked at Elaine searching for an answer.

She shrugged her shoulders, "Sorry it didn't work out."

"You'll get my bill alright," Cavanaugh told Michaelson. "I'll pull my men out now."

"Good. Thank you," Michaelson said.

Miles made a quick grab for Angela's phone, but Elaine was quicker and smashed Miles' wrist with the bottom of her fist before he could reach it. He groaned in pain. Cavanaugh turned to see Elaine knee Miles in the face knocking him to the floor.

"What the hell?" Cavanaugh yelled.

"Oh, my god," Angela said, quickly kneeling down next to Miles.

"She broke my wrist," Miles groaned.

Angela moved into him with her mouth next to his ear and whispered. "You shouldn't have bothered. I sent the text." And she had. When Hobbs and Costa were pulling her down the hall, she reached into her purse, saw the lit send button and hit it.

Miles made a painful grin and whispered. "Work my neck. Not my lips."

"What's he saying?" Michaelson asked.

"Hey, this isn't right," Cavanaugh said.

"Go home, Steve," Elaine said. "I'll call you later and explain."

Cavanaugh looked at her, Michaelson, and the couple on the floor. He made a stupefied nod, shook his head, motioned to his two men to follow him. All three headed out the door. In the hall, he spoke into his lapel mic, "Hey guys. Listen up. It's Cavanaugh. We're done here. Let's stand down and meet in the driveway."

Michaelson moved around his desk, pushing Elaine aside. "Pick them up," he ordered Costa and Hobbs. They reached down and yanked the pair of intruders to their feet. "I know you're not doing this alone," Michaelson said. "How many does George have waiting for you?"

"Hey man," Miles said, holding his wrist. "All I can tell you is that there's fifty FBI men surrounding this house as we speak."

"No one's shown up on our monitors," Michaelson said. "So I don't believe you."

Knowing he might be dead soon and never able to resist a straight-line, Miles said, in a high-pitched voice, "Would you believe twenty?"

Costa hit him in the stomach bending him over the desk gasping for air.

"Mr. M," Elaine said. "If George has men waiting, we'd better get those seven men back."

"I don't want outsiders involved in this. I should have thought when you hired them."

"A show of force will keep anyone away from the house, especially with that dog out there."

Michaelson took a deep breath and let it out. "Okay. Bring them back in."

Elaine hurried out the door, ran down the hall and up the stairs. Veronica who was talking with a couple of the guests saw Elaine running to the front door and wondered what her urgency was. So did Lyedecker and Vereti, but they held their assigned positions keeping their eyes peeled.

Outside on the driveway, Elaine caught up with Cavanaugh as he was assembling his men to leave. "Hey. Michaelson wants you to stay."

"What?"

"Yeah. He apologizes and wants you to finish out the afternoon."

Cavanaugh looked around at his men, thinking and shaking his head. "Okay. Back to your stations and ..." Gunshots coming from the back of the house rang out. "What the hell?"

Elaine pulled out her pistol and ran into the house.

In the back of the house, the two guards on the upper balcony were firing down on George, Chang, Dillon and Gomez, who were taking cover behind a large wooden gazebo.

"On three we jump out and rapid fire at them till our clips are empty," George said. "Chang, you and I take the one on the left. Gomez and Dillon, the right one."

"Right, got it, okay," the three said in unison.

On three, the four jumped out. The two on the balcony could not escape the hail of bullets from four rapid firing pistols. The upper balcony was clear, for the moment.

Fresh clips slapped in, George and Chang charged straight to the lower balcony which, surprisingly to them, was also clear as Hobbs and Costa had left their posts and were in Michaelson's office.

Dillon and Gomez worked their way to the side of the house as planned.

By this time, Elaine had made it through the screaming, panicking crowd trying to exit the living room, and got down the stairs pistol in hand. She ran into Michaelson's office ready to protect him. "I heard shooting."

"I'm okay in here," Michaelson said pulling a pistol from his drawer and pointing it at Miles and Angela. Motioning to Hobbs and Costa he told Elaine, "Take these two and stop whoever's out there."

"Alive?"

"Dead."

Elaine turned and ran back out, followed by Hobbs and Costa. "Your friends, no doubt," Michaelson said to Miles and Angela.

Climbing over the railing of the lower balcony, George and Chang crouched down and looked through the open glass door to see who might be waiting for them.

Elaine, Hobbs and Costa came out of the hall and into the room below the stairs. They saw Chang and George on the balcony and began firing at them shattering the glass door.

George and Chang dropped to the floor with the glass falling around them. Their continued automatic fire, sent Elaine, Hobbs and Costa, bloodied to the floor motionless.

Hearing the shots, Michaelson panicked and momentarily turned his back on Miles and Angela to look down the hall. Miles took that moment to charge him, bad wrist and all. He rammed his shoulder into Michaelson's lower back, propelling him across the hall into the wall. Miles fell to the floor half-way into the hall, then scrambled to his feet to get back into the room. Angela jumped to the door. Once Miles was back inside, she slammed it shut and locked it.

"Move away from the door," Miles yelled.

Angela did, just as three bullets from Michaelson's pistol came through the mahogany door, sending splinters into the room.

In the hall, knowing his blind shots at the door were useless, Michaelson aimed his pistol down the hallway were Elaine, Hobbs and Costa lay dead. He saw no one else, but since the attack was coming from that direction, he turned and headed for a bedroom at the other end of the hall. He ran in, closed the door quietly and locked it.

Upstairs, Veronica gathered up Connie, Odina and Little Bird amongst the scattering guests. She quickly moved them toward the hall at the end of the living room making sure her doll didn't fall out of the bag. "You," she yelled at Freddie. "Come with us."

Freddie, who had his pistol drawn at the front door watching the screaming guests run out, did as ordered and followed Veronica down the hall with Connie, Odina and Little Bird. Veronica pushed her three friends into a room and joined them leaving, Freddie out in the hall. "No one comes down this hall," she told him.

"Right."

She slammed the door shut and locked it.

With Michaelson locked in downstairs, Veronica and friends locked in upstairs with Freddie guarding, it became the same old type of war; the instigators protected, their soldiers fighting and dying.

Coming around the side of the house to the front, Gomez and Dillon surprised the guard with the German Shepard who turned to fire on them. Gomez and Dillon knelt and fired three times each sending the guard flying backwards, his dead hand releasing the leash gave the dog freedom to attack his handler's killers. It ran full speed, straight toward Dillon, growling and baring its teeth. Two other guys, not from the streets, might have been too sensitive to harm an animal and hesitate firing, losing fingers or a hand. These two ex-street boys were in no such peril. The dog never reached them.

"Angela," Chang called out, coming down the lower hall with George behind him.

"Yes," Angela's voice came faintly. "We're down here."

Chang saw a door down the hall on the right open a crack. Angela's voice was louder. "Miles and I are here."

Before Chang and George got to the room, they heard at least two men coming quickly down the stairs. "Don't come out," Chang yelled to Angela as he and George turned toward the stairs and fell to the carpet. They readied their pistols to fire once they could identify the men as not Gomez or Dillon.

Lyedecker and Veretti came running down the stairs into the room. Lyedecker tripped over Elaine's body. Gunfire from George and Chang made sure he didn't get up.

Veretti fired a shot at them and then turned to take cover. Two bullets from George's pistol hit Veretti in the back sending him flying headfirst into the wall. Chang fired, also hitting him in the back. Veretti was dead by the time he bounced back to the floor to join Lyedecker, Elaine, Costa and Hobbs.

Gomez and Dillon approached the front of the house with guests still streaming out of the front door. They found it hard to get clear shots at the two security men who were there. One of them was Cavanaugh who wondered what the hell this altercation was about. Eight years of security work and he never had to draw his pistol. Now it was drawn. But he couldn't get a clear shot through the crowd at the two men who he saw kill his employee and dog.

Cavanaugh's man next to him was not so particular about shooting through a crowd to protect himself. He shot at Gomez as the crowd rushed through his line of fire. His bullet ended up in the back of a grey-haired man in a tuxedo, who, falling to the pavement, now wished he had just coasted along with his senatorial power, instead of reaching for world power.

Gomez saw a beautiful blond girl with a red blouse running with the crowd just before she got hit in the side of the face with the man's second bullet. She fell to the concrete motionless.

"*Pendejo*," Gomez yelled at her killer.

Dillon worked his way to the other side of the running crowd managing to target the girls' killer. One of his three bullets caught the man in the ear. Cavanaugh, now alone, ran into the house as two of Dillon's bullets hit the door frame.

Chang's sister Emma, smart enough not to run into the noise of the outside gunfire, ran into the large kitchen at the back of the living room, grabbed a knife off the drain and hid under the kitchen table.

Downstairs, the hallway cleared, George and Chang joined up with Angela and Miles. She was never so glad to see her husband, including that time in the fog. He pulled out an extra pistol and slapped it into his wife's hand. "Safety's off. Just aim and pull the trigger when you have to."

"I've got the goods," Miles said, holding up the laptop with his good hand.

George pulled out an extra pistol for Miles. "Take this. Safety's off."

Miles shoved the laptop under his right armpit and held it tight under his arm. He grabbed the pistol with his good hand.

"I say go back the way we came to protect these two," George said. "We can meet up with Gomez and Dillon later."

"No way," Chang countered. "Follow the plan. Meet up with them and head to the car. They'll have the way cleared."

"I hope so," George said as he turned to check down the hall, not knowing that Michaelson was in the room to the right of him. "It's clear. Let's hit it." With both hands on his automatic, George lead the three others down the hall toward the stairs.

Chang kept Angela behind him. Miles made sure to keep the laptop secure with his arm. George peered around the corner and up the staircase. It was clear for the moment. He walked up the stair in a crouch, his pistol proceeding him. Chang, Angela and Miles stayed close behind.

Freddie, down the hall, still guarding the four women as ordered, saw the four intruders, pistols at the ready, coming up the stairs. He ran at them firing with unsteady hands, his bullets hitting the railing next to George who ducked down. Chang moved up on the stairs over George and fired three times at Freddie, sending all three bullets to their target.

Is that the Madison Square Garden crowd cheering me? Freddie asked himself. *Yes, I finally made it to WrestleMania.* He hit the mat for the last time.

Cavanaugh, with his six men and dog now dead, came around the corner firing and hitting Chang in his vest. Angela screamed as he fell back onto George. She raised her pistol. Her fire at Cavanaugh, joined by Miles', put the last of the baker's half dozen out of commission, permanently.

Angela turned to her husband lying on top of George. "Are you hit?"

"Cracked rib, probably," Chang said getting to his feet and helping George up. Chang moved forward in front of Angela and Miles to check the front door. "It's looks clear. Let's go." Chang headed toward it, followed by Angela and Miles with George protecting the rear.

Chang cautiously stepped outside, his pistol readied. He saw Dillon and Gomez on guard and waiting as planned.

"It's clear, I think," Gomez said.

"You think?" Chang challenged his friend.

"Yes, I think."

"Good enough," Chang said.

The six proceeded carefully down the driveway. George came upon the red blouse and the long blond hair of a body lying on the driveway. It stopped him cold. He knew it was Judy. He had only been with her that one night, but still the sight of her lying there sickened him.

"Let's go," Chang yelled. George caught up to him, Angela, Miles, Dillon and Gomez heading down the hill to the planned extraction point.

"Still got the laptop, Miles?" George asked, trotting next to him.

"What do you think this is?" Miles said, pulling back his jacket. "A ham sandwich?"

When Michaelson and Veronica heard the gunfire cease, they came out from their separate hiding rooms. Michaelson ran to his office and saw his laptop was gone. Running down the hallway, he ran into the bodies of Elaine and his guards. He quickly reached down and grabbed two of their dropped guns and several ammo clips off Hobbs' belt, stuffed them in his jacket, and ran upstairs.

In the living room, Michaelson met Veronica and her friends coming down the hall. Emma came out of the kitchen still holding the knife. "I saw four of them run out the door just now," Emma reported.

"Was your brother one of them?" Michaelson asked.

"Yeah, I saw the prick. There were four of them. They all had weapons."

"Did you see my laptop with one of them?"

"No, it was pretty quick and then they ran outside," Emma said.

"Well, one of them had it for sure," Michaelson said. "And if they get it to the police, we're dead."

Veronica could imagine what was on the laptop that made Michaelson panic. "Grabs some guns," she commanded Michaelson.

"I've got weapons and ammo right here," he said patting his jacket.

"Get your car?" she demanded.

"Elaine always has the keys. She's dead downstairs."

Veronica turned to Odina. "Blond woman downstairs. Elaine. You know her. Get her keys. We'll get in the car."

At the designated cross street two blocks from Michaelson's house, Cathy was waiting in the SUV. She saw George and the five others heading toward her. She was relieved that none were lost.

Michaelson, Veronica and her three women went out into the driveway that was devoid of any people, save for the four dead bodies. Seeing that Michaelson's BMW had only four seats, Veronica made a quick decision. "Michaelson, front passenger, Emma in the back with me. Connie, you and Little Bird start walking and get away from her before any police arrive. Just start walking. When you get ten blocks from here, call an Uber and get to a hotel. Let me know where you are, and we'll meet later."

"We shouldn't be separated," Connie objected.

"Yeah," Little Bird agreed.

"Move," Veronica said harshly. "Get out of her now."

Connie and Little Bird gave no further complaint, turned and headed down the driveway at a fast walk paying no attention to the bodies of two guards, Judy, the senator or the German Shepard.

"Got the key," Odina said running out of the house.

"Jump in and let's go," Veronica demanded. All four of then got into the BMW and sped off in search of the laptop and the raiders who stole it.

From the top of the hill, Michaelson could see down the long descending street which revealed a white SUV pulling away from the curb in the distance.

"There goes those pricks now," Michaelson said. "That SUV pulling out into the street. That has to be them."

"I see them," Odina said.

"Follow them, but stay back," Veronica said.

"What?" Michaelson objected. "We have to get that laptop. It's got our members' names, stock transactions and more."

"Don't you think I know that?" Veronica said. "If they get close to a police department we kill all of them before they get out of the car. Otherwise, I want to see where they go to have leverage on them. Their friends and relatives. The best way to completely control people."

146

"You're right, Veronica," Michaelson said as he pulled the two automatic pistols and ammo clips out of his jacket. He turned to Emma in the back seat and handed her a pistol. "Okay, here's the deal."

"Yes," Emma said, ready to prove her worth.

"It's up to you and I to get that laptop back and kill those people. All of them. That's imperative. Nothing else matters. Only that."

"I understand," Emma said.

"Now, our two guests here," Michaelson said, motioning to Odina and Veronica, "will drive and advise. But we're the ones that have to get our hands dirty. Elanie, Lyedecker, Veretti and all are dead. There's no one else. You understand?"

"I do," Emma said, "You can count on me."

"Have you ever fired a pistol?"

"Sure. I had a couple of boyfriends who were into guns and let me fire them. I'm from Chinatown. I've seen a couple of guys get dropped. I can handle myself."

"Good," Michaelson said, handing her three ammo clips. "If you get my laptop back and kill those men, I'll make you my chief of security," he lied convincingly.

Emma's eyes lit up. "I'd like that a lot," she said, putting the clips in her jacket pocket.

"Good. Now, this is the second time your brother invaded my home. I want him dead. Especially him. Do you have a problem killing him?"

"My ex-con, asshole brother came into my nightclub, dislocated my bouncer's shoulder and slapped me in the face. Slapped me hard. I'd have a problem not killing him."

While they talked, neither Michaelson nor Emma noticed Veronica's hand moving into her bag. It found its way under her doll's clothes. She felt for the crystal given by her celestial mentor and found it. She moved her hand so that her palm was directly on it and focused her mind.

Emma looked at Veronica as her face reddened from concentration. "Are you okay?"

"Don't talk," Veronica commanded. "Nobody talk. Just follow them at a distance."

CHAPTER 16

1

"I think we've got company," Cathy said, looking into her side mirror. "It looks like we've got Michaelson on our tail."

"What?" George reacted sitting next to her in the SUV. "I thought we got out of there fast enough."

"I told you that our pickup point was too far from the house," Chang complained from the back seat.

"Easy now," Angela said, sitting next to him. "We were lucky to get out of there."

"We're not 'out of there', yet," Chang clarified.

"That's for sure," Miles said still gripping the laptop tightly.

Gomez and Dillon turned in their seats to look out the back window. "I see a copper colored BMW with a black hood," Gomez said.

"That's them," Chang said. "We put a couple of bullet holes in it last time they chased us."

"If it's them," Dillon said. "Something ain't right."

"What do you mean?" asked Gomez. "They're on us all right."

Dillion shook his head. "Yeah, but funny thing." He paused to watch.

"What?" Gomez asked.

"Look. They're not catching up. It's like they're tailing us or something," Dillon said.

"Yeah. You might be right," Gomez said.

"What's their game?" Chang asked.

"Their game," Gomez offered, "is that they're probably calling in more help to join them.

Chang turned to look. "They might already have another carload of men following behind them now."

"Maybe so," Dillon said.

"Whatever they're doing," George said, "we proceed as planned." He pulled out his phone and punched a name.

Patrico was just tying up his boat to the same pier where he had dropped off his four runaway passengers nine days before. He had received a text from George, the day before the raid on Michaelson's house, to meet there at 4 p.m. Now his phone rang.

"Yeah, George. Are you coming?"

"We're on our way now. Be there in forty minutes."

"Did you bring my money?"

"Yes, you'll be paid in full once you get us to Vancouver."

"I'll be paid in full before you get on my boat."

"Sure. Anything you want, except we've got some heat after us, so be ready to shove off fast."

"Yeah. When ain't you had some heat on you for one of your cruises."

"It's 3:50 now. So look for us just before 5:00."

"It'll be dark by then, so look for my flashlight."

"Right."

"And don't drop my money."

2

For the entire forty-minute trip, driving just above the speed limit, Michaelson's BMW kept a steady distance of 150 yards behind the SUV that held the home invaders with his laptop. It was dark now, making it easier for Odina to see their prey's car with its lights on.

"They're turning off up ahead," Odina said.

"Yes," Michaelson said. "Good. I was worried we'd end up at the Canada border and have to deal with that." He turned back to look at Veronica. Her face showed she was still trance-like, her hand still inside her doll. He shook his head in puzzlement and turned back facing front to see the single-lane, forest road that they were now on.

In front of them, Michaelson could see the SUV suddenly speed up. "That's it. They're up to something. Catch those sons-of-bitches," he said to Odina.

Veronica came out of her trance. "Yes. Now you can catch them and kill them."

"Way ahead of you," Michaelson ventured. *Welcome back to the real world*, he thought, but dare not say. He turned back to Emma. "They're heading for the beach and will probably use the same boat as last time. There was just one guy on it. We kill him, too."

"I want George alive," Veronica spoke up.

"What?" Michaelson said.

"Alive," she repeated coldly.

"If possible," Michaelson said.

"Not if possible," Veronica angered. "Shoot him in the arm or the leg, whatever. But he's to be brought back alive."

"I'll see to it personally," Odina said, to her matriarch. "I'll get my hands on one of the dead one's pistol and get the job done."

"All right," Michaelson said to sum up. "George alive. The others, including anyone on the boat, dead."

"Turn here and punch it, Cathy," George said pointing to a dark forest off the road.

"Here? There's no here. Just trees."

"Right. Weave your way through. It'll take us to the pier. I remember it from when we were here."

Cathy turned the SUV sharply hitting a bump, bouncing her six passengers violently. "I hope your memory is good," Cathy said turning on the car's high beams.

"My memory is especially good. Just as yours should be by now."

"Oh, yeah. Right."

"You have the same power, so ..."

"I didn't want it," Cathy said. But you ..."

"Use it to drive like hell and lose those killers behind us."

Cathy swerved to miss a tree.

"You know when we get to Vancouver, we ...."

"Just let me drive, you bastard," she said, seeing an open space between two trees and flooring the accelerator.

"There's not enough space," Angela yelled out.

Cathy kept her foot to the floor, her enhanced mind transmitting calculations to her hands on the wheel.

The SUV barely made it, knocking bark off both trees.

"*Santa mierda, lo hiciste*" cheered a voice behind Cathy. She didn't need an enhanced mind to know who said it.

"Let's see those fuckers behind us try that one."

That had to be Dillon, Cathy thought as she zig-zagged to miss another tree.

George pulled out his phone and punched Patrico's name.

"Yeah," Patrico answered. "Where are you?"

"We're about five minutes from you. Be ready to leave fast and dodge some bullets."

"It's dark as hell with no moon tonight, so look for my flashlight."

"Right."

"You know, I'm not getting paid enough to ..." George punched him off.

He looked back in the car to check out his team. Chang and Angela were at the ready, still pumped up from the raid, as were Dillon and Gomez. Miles' face, however, still transmitted the pain of his broken wrist as he held tight to Michaelson's laptop with his good hand. "How're you doing, Miles?"

"We really stuck it to those bastards, didn't we George?"

"Billy Jack all the way."

"When we get to the beach," Chang said to George, "the two girls run ahead directly to the boat. Agree?"

"Right." George turned to Cathy. "Did you hear that? You and Angela take pistols and run straight to the boat no matter what."

"And if anything happens," Chang added, looking at Angela, "you tell the boatman to take off and get you both to Canada."

"Mr. Gomez," George called out. "Grab that black bag there and pass it up here."

"Here you are," Gomez said, passing it to Chang who gave it to George.

George told Cathy, "When we get out, have your pistol in one hand, this bag in your other. It's got my cash. I've got a lot in my jacket, plus cards in case we get separated."

"Why would we get separated?" Cathy asked.

"Us guys will buy you some cast off time with gunfire until the ..."

"Good," Dillon interrupted, "I'm tired of running from those shits."

"So," George continued to Cathy, "when you and Angela start to cruise off, we jump on board." George looked at Miles. "You go with the girls to the boat."

"I can handle myself," Miles said, "What more do I have to do to proof it?" The SUV bounced over a rock. "Jesus."

"That's not the point, Miles. You've got to protect that laptop. We'll drop you ashore once we're in the clear."

"Okay. I'll get the girls and the laptop to the boat. You can count on that."

"Good."

"Rocks coming up," Cathy said. "The end of the line."

"The boat is about a half mile away," George said. "Can you see them behind us?"

"Yeah, I see their lights," Gomez said. "About two football fields back."

Cathy hit the brakes and the SUV skidded on dead leaves to a stop right next to a boulder.

"Switch off the headlights," George told Cathy.

Cathy hit the switch and grabbed the bag of money as George handed her a pistol. Everyone jumped out.

"The boats straight through there," George said to Cathy, Miles and Angela. "You'll see Patrico's light." The two women took off in a fast walk.

"Hey, slow down," Miles said. "I can barely see anything. I already have a broken wrist. I don't want a broken face to match it."

"That's another one I'll laugh at when we get to the boat," Angela said.

"That wasn't a joke."

George and Chang waited for the three to get a good head start.

"You two take off and cover the women," Gomez said. "Dillon and I will hold this point for a bit, then join you."

"Good," George said. He and Chang took off at a fast walk.

Gomez and Dillion could see Michaelson's approaching car, still with its headlights on.

"Come on you bastards," Gomez said. "I haven't had this much fun since I threw those drunks out of my park."

"You own a park?" Dillon asked as he raised his pistol at the oncoming BMW.

"Yeah, Yellowstone."

"Terrific." Dillon fired two shots.

"Can't do much at this distance," Gomez said, "except hit a tree."

"It'll get us some respect."

"*Es verdad.*" He fired a shot at the approaching car hitting a tree. Then, seeing that George and the group had a good head start he said, "Okay, let's go."

"Already?" Dillon complained.

"Shoot, run, stop, repeat," Gomez said. Guerilla style. "Let's go."

He and Dillon took off to catch up with the others.

"I don't know much about guerilla fighting," Dillon said weaving through the trees in the dark.

"I do," Gomez said. "Revolution tactics is in our blood."

"Street tactics is in mine."

When Dillon and Gomez caught up with George and Chang, the trees were getting denser, so George was using his phone flashlight to guide them through the dark woods.

"Hey, you're gonna mark us," Gomez said to George. "They're right on our tail."

"It's dark as hell in here," Chang said, defending George's actions.

Just then gun shots rang out from behind followed by an instantaneous bullet hitting a tree three feet to their right. "Everyone stay low," George commanded.

"Stay low, my ass," Gomez said. "Turn off that damned light."

George kept it on but lowered it in a crouched position so he could still see the ground to proceed.

"Did you get faint-hearted since getting out of prison?" Chang asked Gomez.

"Hell, no. And I didn't get faint-stupid either, so turn off the damned light." More shots and bullets buzzed by like bees to prove his point.

"We're almost there," George said keeping the light on, "So keep moving."

"Do you see me stopping?" Dillon asked sarcastically bringing up the rear. He stopped and using a tree for cover, fired three quick shots at the flashlight coming after them. The light immediately went out. "That'll slow those mothers down," he said, and then yelled out to them, "I hope you fall on your ass." He turned to catch up with the group.

Miles, Cathy and Angela got to the end of the forest. There was about a hundred yards of open beach between the tree line and the old pier that lead to the boat.

"There's the flashlight," Cathy said.

"Got it," Angela said.

The three headed for Patrico's flashlight in the soft, deep sand that slowed them down to a hard walk.

"I hope he's got coffee on that boat," Miles said. From behind them, gunfire started up. Angela stopped and turned around.

"Let's go," Miles said as he passed her.

Angle didn't move. Miles stopped and looked back to check her. With her black hair and dark clothes, he could hardly see her in the moonless night. "Don't worry, babe," Miles told her. "They'll be along."

Angela hesitated then turned and walked towards Miles. "You know, I'm married, but even so, I never liked 'babe'," she told him, more to lessen her fear by talking, then to teach Miles manners.

"Hey, come on you guys," they heard Cathy call out from the front of the pier.

The two picked up their pace. "We really pulled a ninja in that house, didn't we, Angela?"

"I'll go on any mission with you, Miles."

They reached Cathy at the foot of the pier. Patrico, next to the boat at the end of the pier, now aimed its beam on its rotting boards. "Watch your feet," he called out to the trio.

"Turn off the damned light," Miles yelled to Patrico. It went off.

More gunfire started up. Miles turned his body so that the laptop he was holding under his arm was next to Angela. "Get this aboard," he said. "You too, Cathy. Get aboard."

Angela took the laptop. "What are you going to do?"

"I'll wait and give them some cover. Or at least a distraction."

"You'll be giving them another target, Miles," Cathy said.

"Whatever. Get aboard."

"Well," Angela said. "My husband wanted me aboard, so I'll go." She turned and began taking careful steps on the pier toward the boat.

"I see them," Cathy said.

Angela stopped on the pier and turned to look. It was too dark to see anything but four figures coming out of the tree line and stopping. She could just make out George's blond hair, but she couldn't distinguish her husband from the other two.

"They're all safe," Miles said.

"So far," Cathy whispered like a prayer.

At the tree line, Chang, Dillon, and Gomez were aiming and firing at the gun flashes that were shooting at them in the forest while George was eyeing the stretch of open beach that lay between them and their escape boat. His enhanced eyesight could see the pier with Cathy, Miles, and Angela standing on it. "This isn't going to work if we make a run for it together," George said. "They'll be on us too soon."

"I agree," Chang said, standing behind a tree and aiming his pistol into the dark forest waiting for another gun flash. Next to him, behind trees were Dillon and Gomez, guns at the ready.

"You three, take off," Gomez said. "I'll hold them back. And when you're on the boat, I'll make a run for it."

"No way," Chang said. "We go together."

"Here's where I earn my twenty-five-grand," Gomez said. "Besides, I've got this vest."

"Not on your back," Chang pointed out.

"We're wasting time," Gomez said. "They might have another carload of men join them and be flanking us right now. So take off."

"What do you think, Dillon?" Chang asked his brother as a bullet hit the tree next to him.

"I think it stinks," Dillon said. "But it's the only way."

"Okay, damn it," Chang said. "Take off, Dillon."

"I go when you go," Dillon said. "Remember our Red Dragon Lantern date with the folks?"

George knowing that hesitation would only give their pursuers more time to work their way around them said, "No time for this. Go Gomez. And zigzag."

Knowing not to waste time debating, Gomez took off across the beach. He knew zigzagging would make him harder to hit, but it would also allow a shooter more time to nail him. He chose a beeline straight to the pier, like a bee whose job was done gathering nectar and goes directly back home.

Gomez's crummy home was nothing for him to look forward to. But now that he had given his daughter twenty of the twenty-five thousand dollars, he had some of his daughter's respect back. Maybe she would eventually invite him to her home for an extended visit if he made it to the boat. If they all sailed off clean.

A bullet buzzed by Gomez's head, sounding like a bee heading home.

At the tree line, George, Dillon, and Chang continued firing shots into the forest to give Gomez cover. One of their bullets, by sheer chance, found home in Odina's head as she followed Michaelson and Emma through the forest with Veronica behind her.

155

When they heard the crunch of the bullet and the sound of Odina's body hitting the dead leaves on the ground, Michaelson and Emma hid behind trees, then turned and looked back.

Even with their eyes now adjusted to the darkness, they could barely make out Veronica behind them. She kept walking, approaching where Odina fell. Another woman, when seeing her childhood friend shot dead, would have fallen to her knees and wept. But another woman would have been of this earth. Veronica stepped over Odina without a downward look.

"Gomez made it," George said to Dillon and Chang.

"Okay, then take off," Chang said as a bullet hit the tree he was hiding behind.

George started running in a crouch. He zigzagged twice then the truth and the fear hit him. More time as a target. So he headed straight to the pier. Even with his enhanced powers the deep, soft sand slowed him down. But he didn't need enhanced hearing when Cathy yelled out, "Come on, you bastard."

George could see Gomez and Miles standing next to her with Angela behind them on the middle of the pier, while Patrico stood next to the boat.

Finally, George made it to them at the pier.

"Thank God," Cathy said.

George turned to look back at the tree line to see if Chang and Dillon had started their run. But they hadn't.

"Are you hit, George?" Cathy asked.

"I'm good. You should get on the boat."

"What about you?" she asked.

George looked at Miles. "Get Cathy and Angela on the boat. Mr. Gomez and I will cover the Chang and Dillon."

"All right," Miles said, knowing that it was the right strategy for the situation.

"I see you still have the ham sandwich," George said to Miles.

"Yeah," Miles said, holding up the laptop. "Hopefully with lots of names and criminal activity on it."

"Where's my husband?" Angela called out behind them, still standing on the middle of the pier.

"He's coming," George called back. "You three get on the boat," he said to her as Cathy and Miles slowly worked their way towards her on the pier.

Back at the tree line Dillon and Chang were firing into the forest. Suddenly, Chang heard his brother yell out. He turned to see Dillon fall back onto the sand.

"Jesus," Chang said, diving down next to him. "Where did you get hit?"

"Right thigh."

"All right. The hell with this. Let's get out of here together."

"I'm with that."

"Come on." Chang put his left arm around Dillon's back and slowly helped him to his feet. "I'm going to empty my clip at them, and then we make a run for it. Right?"

"I'll go as fast as I can."

Chang fired five quick shots into the forest until he clicked empty. "Let's go." He put his pistol in his jacket pocket, his arm around Dillon and guided him forward.

Chang could still feel the pain of his old shoulder wound but chose to ignore it. The soft sand fought against them, making each step for Dillon painfully slow, even with the fear adrenaline coursing through him.

"There they are," George said, standing next to Gomez. "They're coming," he called to Patrico. "Cast off."

Patrico started untying the ropes from the pier as Cathy, Angela, and Miles reached the boat.

Chang and Dillon had only gone a few yards on the beach, when Dillon took a bad step and fell, bringing both men down to the sand.

"Come on, get up," Chang said as he stood grabbing Dillon's belt.

Emma came running out of the forest. She saw Chang trying to stand Dillon up, giving her time to steady her pistol in both hands. Aiming at her brother's back she fired twice. One bullet hit the back of Chang's arm spinning him down to the sand.

From the pier, Angela saw the brothers fall. She sprang forward at a run, but after five steps a rotten board splintered halfway through, throwing her forward and down onto the pier.

George and Chang took off running toward the two fallen men as they saw Emma approaching them, now struggling to get to their feet. George and Dillon's only hope was to get off a lucky shot before Emma fired at Chang.

Angela, though stunned, got to her feet and began walking the rest of the pier to the beach.

"Come back," Patrico called to Angela.

Cathy and Miles got off the boat to go after Angela.

"Are you hit?" Dillon asked Chang.

"My arm. Same damned place as last time. Let's go." He turned over on his side to get up, when he saw his sister step into view, pistol pointed down at him.

"You wanna slap me again?" Emma said.

Emma heard George's voice yell out, "No, don't."

From behind Emma, Michaelson walked up.

"Head of security guaranteed?" Emma asked Michaelson but knew the answer.

"Guaranteed," Michaelson lied again.

Chang struggled to get up. Dillon tried to reach for his pistol that lay under him. George knelt on the sand and raised his pistol at Emma knowing his enhanced mind would guide his aim. Gomez stopped next to him.

Suddenly, a loud, booming hum sounded as the beach was lit up with an intense greenish, light. Everyone froze and looked up as the entire beach from tree line to pier was now bathed in the supernatural light coming from above.

Emma, now paralyzed with the fear of God in her, relaxed her finger on the trigger of her pistol. "What the hell?" she said, as she let her pistol hand hang down.

Michaelson looked up. "It's true," he said in awe. "It's all true."

From the pier, still in darkness, Cathy and Angela watched the six people out there in a large circular beam that made them look like they were playing out a Greek tragedy in a lit-up theater-in-the-round.

George, in the outer edge of the bright circle of concentrated light, kneeling next to Gomez, looked up to see where the light was coming from.

Gomez knew that a prisoner can still kill you, even when a prison siren goes off. So, wherever that light and sound was coming from, he didn't give a shit. Kneeling in the sand, with the bright light on his two targets, he concentrated on the two brother's survival by keeping his gun pointed at Michelson and Emma. If they made a bad move, he would fire. And whatever was overhead lighting up the place like a searchlight in a night prison escape was not important at the moment.

Finally, Michaelson recovered from his shock of the thing from above and got back to the purpose. "Kill them both," he told Emma as Chang looked up at them knowing his pistol was empty. Dillon grabbed his gun that was under him.

"God is watching us," Emma said under the intense green light.

"That's not God," Michaelson said. "That's our leader who ..."

Just then, Dillon got a hold of his gun and started to slowly roll over. Seeing this, Michaelson raised his gun at Dillon. The three rapidly fired bullets from Gomez's gun knocked Michaelson six feet back on the sand, dead.

Seeing that, and knowing she was next, Emma let her gun fall to the sand and raised her hands up.

"She's weaponless now," Gomez said to George, "but just say the word."

"Negative," George said. "but stay on her just in case."

"Right."

Recognizing his sister in the bright light, Dillon said loudly over the oscillating hum, "Emma? You're Emma. What are you doing here?"

"Going bad," Chang said.

"What the hell is up there?" Emma asked, looking up in awe.

"Like you said, Emma," Chang said getting to his feet, "God is watching us." He reached down to help Dillon. "So go and sin no more less a greater sin come upon you."

"Jesus, Chang," Dillon said, getting to his feet. "You never went to church."

"Prison chapel, last three years," Chang said.

George and Gomez approached. "Let's get the hell out of here," Gomez said. "before that thing up there zaps us."

"Yeah, good idea," Chang said.

Angela, Cathy and Miles joined the group, as Emma started backing away. She turned and started walking toward the tree line.

"Hey, Emma," Dillon called out over the hum. "We're taking the folks to the Red Dragon Lantern. We'll call you."

"Are you serious?" Chang asked, in pain from his wounded arm.

"Yeah, why not?" Dillon answered, also in pain from the bullet in his leg.

Emma didn't react. She walked back into the forest where the BMW was parked.

As the group saw Emma walking into the forest out of the light, they saw Veronica walk out of the forest into the light. She stopped at the tree line and stood there motionless. She looked up to the source of the light, seemingly not minding its intensity.

"What the hell is this?" George said. "She's alive."

"Yeah, George," Miles said. "In all this excitement it slipped my mind that the Indian girl from San Francisco was at the party today. It turns out she's the big cheese."

Ignoring Miles, George said, "Everyone get to the boat. I'll be there soon."

"What do you think you're going to do, George?" Cathy asked harshly.

"Just go to the boat so we can get away from this damn UFO," George said.

"Stay away from her, George," Cathy demanded.

"Let's get away from this place," Dillon said.

"Right," Chang said. The two wounded brothers and Angela started walking to the pier.

Cathy shook her head. "The hell with him. Get me out of here."

George didn't respond and started walking toward Veronica.

Cathy turned toward the boat and started walking with the others.

"All right," Gomez said turning and following. "Let's get on the boat and take off. With or without him."

The six slowly headed to the boat. Every few steps one of them would stop to look up at the thing that was lighting their way. But all they could see past the intense light was the shape of some massive, dark, circular object.

As George approached the still motionless Veronica, he looked at her hands for a weapon, but she only held her bag with the doll in it. She was still l looking upwards, the green light making Veronica look unearthly. As George stopped in front of her, she turned her attention from what hovered above them, to look at George.

"I thought I killed you," George said.

"It didn't take," she said calmly.

"Michaelson's dead."

"It doesn't matter."

George looked up shielding some of the intense light with his hand. "What is that up there?"

"Transport."

He looked back at her. "Are you giving up and leaving?"

"Nothing can stop what we started. So we'll just leave you all to yourselves. We'll come back when you're at your weakest."

"We'll see about that," George said calmly.

"Too bad you didn't get to the next level, George."

"What's that level?"

"You would have lik ..."

A beam of circular white light, amidst the green light, shot down touching Veronica's head. A flash of a green cyclone-shaped light seemed to be sucked out of her head and shoot upwards. Her body fell lifeless to the sand. George jumped down to catch her before her head hit. The humming got louder, the green light gradually diminished to nothing. Holding Veronica in his arms now in darkness, George looked up to see the large, dark circular shape ascending.

On the boat that was still at the pier, Cathy, Chang, Angela, Miles, Gomez, and Patrico watched the dark shape disappear. "I'm glad that thing's gone," Miles said. "Gives me the creeps."

"Yeah," Gomez said. "But what the hell was it?"

Angela was seeing to Chang's and Dillon's wounds as best she could. "You got a first aid kit?" she asked Patrico.

"Yeah, in the cabin, on the wall."

"I'll get it," Gomez said and went into the cabin.

"I'll be alright," Dillon said. "Let's cast off and get some space between us and this damn beach."

"What about George," Miles said, staring at the now dark beach.

"He can handle himself," Chang said.

"I'll call him," Cathy said pulling out her phone and punching his name. Four rings and there was no answer. Six rings and no answer. "Come on, George, answer," she said looking at her phone display.

Gomez came out of the cabin with the first aid kit and handed it to Angela. He looked to see the group looking out toward the beach. "What's going on"?

"Hey. I hear a phone," Miles said.

"It's coming from out there," Patrico said, pointing to the dark beach. "It's ringing."

"It's him," Cathy said relieved. "Coming closer."

All six of them looked out at the beach and soon saw George coming out of the darkness, carrying the lifeless Veronica is his arms. On her stomach was her bag and doll. The ringing sound of George's phone could be heard in his pocket. He started walking carefully on the pier.

Cathy punched off her call to him. "Oh, my god," she said, seeing Veronica's body. "He just can't leave her."

"Hey, Patrico," George called out. "Why didn't you tell me that you didn't dump her."

"Hey man. I didn't know what to think," Patrico called back. "I got up to throw her overboard that day and all I saw was the sheet we wrapped her in. So I weighted that and deep-sixed it."

"Well, what did you think happened to her?" George asked.

"I didn't know what to think. She was dead and then she was gone. So I just cruised back to Seattle."

"Well, here she is again," George said, approaching the boat. "Maybe you can give it another try."

"I will if you give me my money."

George stepped aboard. "I have it." He laid Veronica's body down on the deck bench and stood over it for a moment as Cathy watched him.

"You're still calling the shots, George," Miles said impatiently. "Are we cruising off or what?"

George turned away from Veronica. "Maybe not," George told him.

"Now what are you thinking?" Cathy asked George.

"Maybe we don't have to go," George said to her.

"So what do we do?" she asked.

"Mr. Gomez," George said. "The bullets from your pistol are in Michaelson's body out there, so put your pistol in this bag," he said pointing to Veronica's doll bag. "It'll go overboard along with her and her father."

"Father?" Gomez asked.

"Her doll," Patrico said.

Gomez put his pistol into Veronica's bag. "Yeah, we just might get away with this when they find his body, as long as we're not around."

Chang stood up. "What do you think?" he asked George. "Is it all clear for a while."

"Yeah," George said. "I think so. Especially now that we've got the laptop. So let's all work our way back to the SUV and ..."

"What about my money?" Patrico asked.

"I got it right here, already counted out," George said. He turned to the others and said, "Okay. Now that Michaelson and Veronica here are both ... no longer a problem, I think we're safe for a while. So let's get back to the SUV and get this laptop to the right people."

"Sounds good to me," Miles said.

Chang turned to his brother, and though wounded himself, helped him to his feet. George pulled out a wad of cash he had prepared for Patrico and put it in his hand. "It's a little more than I promised."

"Good," Patrico said. "I deserve it."

"Good luck with the deep-sixing this time," George told him.

"I'll get it done for sure this time," Patrico said. "I guess that UFO had something to do with her disappearing off my boat in the first place."

"Don't look at me to explain the unexplainable," George said.

"Oh, wait a minute," Patrico said befuddled. "She was dead. What the hell?" He shook his head and started thumbing through the cash.

Cathy passed George on her way off the boat. "Let's go, George."

"You still feel like driving?" he asked her.

"Yeah, I guess so," she answered, calmly stepping onto the pier and turning on her phone flashlight.

"There's a broken board ahead," Angela warned. "So be careful."

"*Hijole*," Gomez said stepping off the boat. "You guys get into some crazy shit."

George looked at the wounded brothers getting off the boat with Angela's help and said, "Well, let's go wake up the dog doctor."

CHAPTER 17

1

The next day, a few miles south of the beach where the three deaths took place, an Uber car pulled up to a large cabin in the woods. The owner having heard it approach and not expecting anyone came outside on his deck to see who it was.

He saw two beautiful, young Native American women getting out of the car.

"Thank you", one of them who looked familiar to him said to the driver.

"Sure thing," the driver replied and then backed down the driveway.

"Remember me?" the taller one said. "I'm Connie."

"Oh, sure. I met you in Arizona," Don said. "Veronica's friend."

"Right."

"Yeah, right," Don said. "What was that business passing me on the road and throwing by suitcase at me?"

"Oh," Connie smiled. "Veronica put me up to it. You know her. Kind of pushy."

"To say the least," Don agreed. "How did you find me?"

"You gave me your name, location and an invitation to come see you. Remember?"

"Yeah, I remember. But I meant when I thought Veronica would be with me."

"Well, she's not here," Connie said. "This is my friend Little Bird."

"Hello, Little Bird," Don said, still puzzled by this surprise visit. "I like your name."

Little Bird smiled. "You're the first guy to say that to me."

"Oh, I doubt that," Don said smiling.

"You're the first one."

"Well, it's good to be first."

"So," Connie said. "How about it?"

"Oh. Sure. Come on in. I could use the company?"

The two women smiled as they walked up the stairs to the deck. "Little Bird is a little hungry, Connie said."Could you give her something ... anything to eat?"

"It's still morning," Don said. "So how does bacon, eggs and toast sound?"

"Some coffee, too?" Little Bird asked.

"I've got instant," he said holding the screen door open for them.

"That's fine with us," Connie said entering the cabin.

"Make yourself at home," he said.

Suddenly, a large fly buzzed him. With lightning speed his hand whipped out and grabbed it, surprising himself.

2

A few days later, in a San Diego home a young nude woman gasped for air, pushed her lover aside and crawled to the edge of the bed to catch her breath. Crawling too far, she slowly slid down the blankets to the floor.

Breathing heavily, she struggled to get herself to a sitting position and leaned back on the bed. Looking over to the nightstand she saw her alarm clock. Not wearing her glasses when making love, she couldn't quite make out the time.

Struggling, she leaned over, reached up and grabbed it. She held it in front of her face and then held it up to give to her boyfriend.

He sat up without the exhaustion his girlfriend had and took it with a puzzled expression. "It's 4:25 in the morning," he said. "So what?"

"So what? Do you know what time we started?"

"I don't know."

"Okay. Tell me right now what you're taking?" she demanded.

"What do you mean? I'm not taking anything, if you're talking about drugs or something."

"No, you're taking something," she insisted. "Ever since you came back from your trip, you hardly ever sleep, you know most of the answers on *Jeopardy* and *Wheel of Fortune* and you bang me for hours. What happened to you?"

"I don't know," he shrugged. "Maybe it's from drinking that Mount Shasta water."

END

ABOUT THE AUTHOR

At age 8, Paul saw *The Making of 20,000 Leagues Under the Sea* and decided to make movies. Age 18, his 16mm, 30-minute action movie ***Trapped*** wins the Berkeley Film Festival. Paul graduates from San Francisco State University with a BA in Film Production.

In the USAF, he films space launches for NASA. His first feature film ***The Tournament*** was filmed in 35mm Techniscope. The story of three samurai going to England to enter a fencing tournament. Now an extra on the Blu-ray of his movie 'Ninja Busters'.

Paul writes & directs ***Death Machines***. It's distributed by Crown International Pictures, opening in 50 theaters in Southern California.

Writes & Directs ***Weapons of Death***. It plays around the world, breaking house records in New York & San Francisco.

His action/comedy ***Ninja Busters*** is on Blu-ray with the director's commentary. Next came the crime story One Way Out.

Wrote & directed **Omega Cop**, starring Adam 'Batman' West, Troy Donahue & Stuart Whitman.

Wrote & produced **Rock Star Rising** audio-book, narrated by Rod Taylor. Performed by Russ Tamblyn, George Chakiris, Robert Culp, James Darren and Kevin McCarthy.

Wrote & directed the largest production in audio-book history: **McKnight's Memory** narrated by Frank Sinatra Jr. Performed by Robert Culp, Nancy Kwan, Don Stroud, Henry Silva, Alan Young, Barbra Leigh, H.M Wynant, David Hedison and Edd Kookie Byrnes.

Paul directed Edd Byrnes' audio-memoir **My Casino Caper**. Edd was stalked for his 3 million-dollar Las Vegas win. Performed by Edd, Alan Young, Henry Silva, David Hedison & Michael Callan.

2018 - He wrote & directed the feature film **Forbidden Power**. Winner of 28 awards at IMDB-sanctioned film festivals, including Best Screenplay at the Florence Film Awards Italy & Best Feature Film at the New York Cinematography Awards.